71

"I am
interested in Margaret,
but I don't really care..."

Margaret Oliver needs to get away to
Aunt Josie's and rest, to think about what
to do with her insensitive, humorless
husband.

But there is no rest—only "dreams" at night
and visions of Josie and her lover, Paul
Tyson, during the day. When suddenly,
Paul's revolutionary explorations into the
action of time approach the breakthrough
point, there is Paul's . . . suicide?
accident? murder?

And all the while her subconscious
is active, restless, goading her on, offering
suggestions, trying to find out what is
happening to Margaret . . . and why?

MARGARET AND I

KATE WILHELM

A TIMESCAPE BOOK
PUBLISHED BY POCKET BOOKS NEW YORK

A Timescape Book published by
POCKET BOOKS, a Simon & Schuster division of
GULF WESTERN CORPORATION
1230 Avenue of the Americas, New York, N.Y. 10020

Published by arrangement with Little, Brown and Company
Library of Congress Catalog Card Number: 70-154951

ISBN: 0-671-83430-4

First Pocket Books printing March, 1978

10   9   8   7   6   5   4   3   2

POCKET and colophon are trademarks of Simon & Schuster.

Printed in the U.S.A.

For Damon — of course

We have no knowledge of how this unconscious functions, but since it is conjectured to be a psychic system it may possibly have everything that consciousness has ... If the unconscious can contain everything that is known to be a function of consciousness, then we are faced with the possibility that it too, like consciousness, possesses a subject, a sort of ego.

Individuation is complete when the conscious and the unconscious learn to *know, respect,* and *accommodate* each other.

C. G. Jung

Chapter 1

Even the subdivisions thinned out after Margaret passed
Brookhaven, and she started to watch for the turnoff, to
her left, that would take her to Josie's house. They say
that there used to be many large estates on this part of the
island and perhaps they were still there, but from the highway they were invisible and, she suspected, long since
abandoned, razed for the innumerable rows of houses and
white concrete streets. It was hot that day; an out-of-season
heat wave had come in to replace April's sooty rains, and
the expressway had been swarming with traffic, apparently
headed toward Jones Beach. They separated, she to hew to
her more northern route, the endless parade keeping right.
Brookhaven. She looked at the signs and what? She
couldn't remember if she thought about it then or not: I
did and have since then, I know. So while I thought about
atomic accidents and mutated brush, purple grasses, white
leaves, disproportionately shaped trees, and such, she was
preoccupied with watching for the turnoff, although it
wasn't even due for twenty miles. Bennett had said twenty
miles. I tried to make her remember his words, but only

succeeded in making her anxious, so I gave up and continued to consider Brookhaven. She was worrying about the narrowness of the road, hoping she wouldn't meet a truck on it. And she had slowed down infernally. Not that I cared particularly. I studied the roadside, and noticed the clouds that were scudding now, and smelled the sea air, and let her worry about trucks.

I began watching for the turnoff, too, and if she missed it, I planned to give her an itch that wouldn't let up for hours.

There were cliffs along her left, Margaret was thinking, with some surprise. Now and then there was a glimpse of the sound, and the air had changed in the past half hour or so, smelling of air that has been purified by hundreds of miles of interplay with salt spray and sun. She drove through Baiting Hollow with absolutely no awareness that in less than a tenth of a mile she would have to turn. I made her hands tighten, and she decided it must be near now. I made her slow down and make the turn, and then keep her eyes on the left to catch the first sight of the house from above it on the road. I could remember the entire scene with Bennett when he described this place, but, of course, she didn't. She was pleasantly jolted when she saw the small gray building in front of boulders that almost dwarfed it, and the scraggly, wind-warped pines that shielded it from the constant sea wind. I shall call it the sea.

The road twisted and the view was gone. She didn't see it again until she made a second turn, this time from the tertiary road that was pitted and gutted, to a driveway that was in even worse condition. It had heaved and cracked and thawed so many times in the past that there were

jumbles of macadam and deep gullies and hummocks of
grasses. It led to the house and was passable, in low, if you
had no need to get back out in a hurry. Margaret thought
that perhaps she would never want to leave. She looked
out the rearview mirror as she slipped and ground her way
toward the house and already she was alone in the world.
The poor road was out of sight; there was nothing but the
boulders and the steep driveway and the house.

It was for the sea that she had come. She sat in the car
when she brought it to a halt and stared out at the choppy
water, blue green, gray, purple, whitecapped and rough at
a shoals several hundred feet offshore, smooth and glassy
on this side of the sandbars, wavelets which hardly even
murmured as they touched the coarse sand shore. She
found herself leaving the car. I took her toward the rocks
that were tossed this way and that, and stood her on them
with the wind whipping her skirt about her legs, feeling
through her the sea and the air and the chill that erased
the thoughts of the heat of the city and the long drive to
this place. She listened to the quiet waves and the rustle of
the grasses as blades rubbed and freed themselves only to
rub abrasively again. It was too late for a swim, already
the shadows were elongated and black, and the air was
cooling very fast. Tomorrow, she promised, herself or the
sea, and she wasn't certain which. Tomorrow.

She opened the house then, not paying more than curso-
ry attention to it yet. She hadn't come for the house.
Bennett had said it was very nice; he said the Metropolitan
Museum was very nice; Buckingham Palace was very nice;
his hotel room in Atlanta from which he had called her
last night was very nice; Josie's house was very nice. Later
she would study it, pry, redecorate it in her mind, but then

she was not interested. She scowled at the thoughts of Bennett that kept bobbing up. She had come here to think about Bennett, but not tonight. Not now.

She took the groceries from the car, studied the remaining driveway to the garage which had an apartment over it, and shook her head. It certainly was impassable. Bennett had told her not to leave the car out where the salt spray and blowing sand would pit the finish, but the driveway was nothing but holes. She turned and glanced at the length she had driven and saw that there really was no difference. She finished unpacking the car, took her bags inside the house and left the car standing outside the door, where the wind would drive salt and sand against it and pit it and pit it and pit it.

Margaret was too tired to think, too tired to care that the house was wrapped in dust covers from end to end. I had her pull the sheets from the furniture and toss them in a corner; if she had no curiosity about the house, I did. I got her started on unpacking the groceries and through her eyes I examined the kitchen. As she put things away I wondered about the house, about Josie, why she had left it like this; I wondered about Bennett, what he was doing, and what Margaret would do next. I didn't care a lot. I am interested, but don't really care, unless she begins to go the route of drugs. I keep her away from them, when I can. Sleeping pills are the worst; they hit me harder than they do her. The others usually don't touch me at all, but they make her try to get at me, sometimes, and that can be bothersome. She is so terribly afraid of me. If it weren't for that those probes wouldn't matter, might even be nice for both of us, but she is afraid of what she'll find, and I can't reassure her without bringing on the acute anxieties that make her reach for the sleeping pills: ourobouros. I wondered: if the worm got enough of his tail inside him, so that it reached the digestive juices, how much of himself would he digest before he died of auto-cannibalism?

Margaret lifted a bottle of bourbon from the last of the bags and stared at it as if she had forgotten that she had packed it herself. Suddenly she sat down hard, still clutching the bottle.

"God," she whispered. "Oh, God, what am I doing?" She felt as if she had been asleep and stared about at the kitchen as if seeing it for the first time that evening. The same thoughts kept going around and around, drowning out everything else: she had to think about Bennett and her; she had to call him before eight; she had to eat something. At the thought of eating she realized that she hadn't eaten since nine that morning, and then only toast and coffee.

Briskly she rummaged among the groceries she had put away in the refrigerator and brought out cold beef, lettuce and tomatoes, and a quart of milk. She was being determined so I left her alone. She made a sandwich and ate it as she wandered again through the house, carrying a glass of milk. Her room, in blue and white, nice ... She said, ugh, at the word nice. He had her doing it. The room was comfortable, feminine, well furnished with a chaise longue, a chair, a large bed, a desk, dresser. A closet was half full of clothes, all in dust bags. She would look them over the next day, she thought, closing the door. A partitioned bathroom led to a second bedroom, and this one was a man's room. She pulled dust covers off to see the furniture. Brown and white, plain, larger than the first bedroom. She wandered through it to the hall, and I gave her a twinge and sent her back to look it over more carefully. She was almost finished with her sandwich, and was thinking about the coffee she had left on the stove. She saw little of the room, but I studied it very carefully. The bed was twin size, covered with a tailored spread; there was a very worn leather chair and a large desk with a drawing board tilted back on it, half a dozen pens in a brown mug. One wall was covered with shelves of books, a print and some blown-up astronomy pictures on another wall ...

Margaret left the room again and once more felt the urge to return. There was something about it ... She shrugged. Tomorrow.

I let her go and looked again at the bedroom, now a permanent part of my memory. It was the best room in the house, with a fireplace between double windows overlooking the sea and the rocks. The room had been used by someone who appreciated it. The leather chair was worn, but kept, probably always in that same spot where he could look up from his book and study the patterns of light and dark on the water. The rug had indentations; the chair belonged there, as the desk belonged where it was, and the ashtray on the desk, and the wastebasket by the desk. A swing-out typewriter? I made her put down her coffee and return to the bedroom and examine the desk more closely; there it was, complete with electric typewriter. She went back to the kitchen and finished eating then.

She was thinking about the room too, and as so often happens when her thoughts echo mine, there was a good bit of carryover. That was the middle ground where I feel that I can almost get through to her, or let her come into me.

She and Bennett had talked of Josie now and then, but she could remember little of what he had told her about his aunt. Josie Oliver was his old maid aunt, he had said jokingly once: Josie Oliver, the famous theater designer.

"She pulled out the year before we got married," Bennett had said. "No one knows why. She never said. But she's in London now, and the house is standing there vacant, and she says that we are welcome to it anytime."

That was all that Margaret could remember of Josie Oliver. But Bennett's old maid aunt holed up in a country house with a man? Who was he, where was he? Why hadn't they married? Margaret frowned, wondering if Bennett knew anything about this. I knew that he didn't. He would never have permitted his wife to come into the house if he had known. The thought made her uneasy and she pushed it aside.

I had a lot more about Josie than she did, but none of it added to any more than she had reached: the pages of Bennett's album that had ads for various shows that Josie had designed sets and costumes for; a few cards she had sent him when he was younger; a note or two. I looked again at her decisive handwriting, bold, self-assured, half script, half print, all her very own. No picture. I never had seen her or a picture of her. Bennett's description: "She's two or three years older than I am"—he was now forty—"rather pretty, or was a few years ago, taller than you, but not very much, thin, smokes like a train, with long skinny fingers. I remembered her fingers. She loved rings, great big flashy ones, wore them all the time. She lost one of them at our house once and there was hell for a week until it was found, turned out that it was a real emerald."

That was Josie. Her room had been stripped of personal

things: her books were gone, her art materials, her accessories had been cleared from the bathroom and the dresser in her room. But his, the man's, things were all there, just as he must have left them. Why? I knew she would hear the telephone ring in a moment or two, and that it was seven-thirty then, and that Margaret had to call Bennett before eight. Also, she was getting cool, and she was afraid to turn on the furnace.

The telephone rang and Margaret jerked at the sound. I would have warned her if I'd been able to. Sometimes I can, but not usually.

"Hello," she said, almost in a whisper, not wanting to hear her own voice in that quiet house.

"Miss Oliver? This is Gus Dyerman. Everything all right up to the house?"

Margaret stared blankly at the phone. Gus Dyerman, the grocer that the agent said would check. Why didn't the fool remember? She didn't, not at all. She made a noise that could have meant anything and he said:

"I wanted to tell you that I put some logs on the back stoop for you. And m'boy Harry'll be there first thing in the morning to light your furnace, less'n you want him to do it tonight. Don't 'spect it'll get very cold tonight though, do you?"

"No, not at all. It's fine," Margaret said. She didn't know what to call him. He had slurred his name and she wasn't even sure of what or who he was.

"Yes'm. If you want anything, want Harry to bring up anything, you just call, you hear? Nice lamb chops came in today, and some good Boston lettuce. ..."

"I don't think, I mean ... Yes, I'll call, if I think of anything. ..."

"Better take down my new number, Miss Oliver. It's 378-9402. You got that?"

"Yes," Margaret said, almost desperately, "but I'm not ..."

"I'll just send up a few things that I recall you used to like, nice berries up from the South, and some cream, and eggs. Anything you don' need, just send back with Harry. Won't bother you no more tonight, Miss Oliver. Glad to have you back again, ma'am."

Margaret sat holding the still phone and finally laughed. "Just what the hell difference does it make?" she said. She would straighten it out the next day, or someday. She glanced at her watch and dialed the hotel in Atlanta where Bennett was staying.

"Hello, dear, I'm here." Margaret forced gaiety into her voice.

"Good. Everything all set then? Is the electricity turned on, the furnace, and everything?"

"Yes. Everything's fine."

"Good. You get some rest and I'll try to get up in the middle of the week. I can't promise yet, though. Did you catch the evening news?"

"No, I forgot ... I was just getting in," she added quickly.

"Okay, but try to get the late news. We made all the networks. Greeley's in great form. Tomorrow we're off to Birmingham. ..."

I could see Bennett, crisp white shirt, black tie, spotless black tuxedo, his hair so precise it might have been painted on. No man named Arnold, I thought at Margaret forcefully, will ever become President. Margaret thought how much she disliked Arnold Greeley; she said, "Let me know where you are in Birmingham. I won't try to call you again. It will be much easier if you just call here from time to time. I'll be here."

Pictures of Bennett flashed on and off in her mind: Bennett smiling at her, his glasses hiding his eyes behind reflections of twin lamps, his lips curved showing his gorgeous teeth. Bennett gorgeous, phoney but gorgeous, right out of a poster of the most successful man of his time, with painted-on hair and eyes that hid behind glasses and teeth that made dentists envious. Bennett turning off the light before touching her. Bennett coming in late, groping for her in the dark, finishing with her quickly, falling asleep, not knowing, or caring, if she slept then, or if she crept from the bed. . . . Bennett, sleeping, mouth partly open, trickle of drool.

"Take care of yourself, darling," he said. "See you next week."

Margaret put the phone down very gently, hardly making a sound. She went to the kitchen and poured bourbon into a glass, added a little water, and drank it quickly. She made a second drink, took it with her to the living room and stared at the television in the corner. The late news. She'd try to remember.

She had to make the bed, and unpack some of the things from her suitcase. The agent had said linens were in drawers; she rummaged until she found them. The blue and white room was cold. She was shivering by the time she had the sheets in place. She had a sweater in one of the suitcases, but she went past them and looked inside the closet again and took a plastic-wrapped sweater from the shelf. It was a pale blue cashmere sweater with crystal buttons. Eighty dollars, she thought, putting it on. She remembered the logs and went out to the back stoop to bring in some of them. On her way back she remembered that there was a fireplace in the brown and white room as well as in the living room, and she turned and went inside the man's room, where she laid the fire and made the bed. She looked inside the closet; his clothes were there.

She took the clothes bag away from his jackets and slacks and felt the rough cloth, and then backed away from them and returned to the living room. She looked over the television-stereo console and put on a record, and as it played she washed her dishes. She took her bags from the blue and white room and put them in the other one. I was pleased with her; I'd barely even nudged her about it. She liked the brown and white room better, too.

She was hardly thinking at all, just doing things without questioning herself, keeping her mind as blank as she could. When she finished with the few things that she had to do, she was lost for several minutes and a feeling of near panic overcame her; it passed quickly as she started to examine the bookshelves in the living room. She pulled down an illustrated *Morte d'Arthur* and took it with her to the bathroom and started to run water into the tub.

I was busy too, not bothering with her at all really. I was sorry that she had chosen the Mallory book. I knew it already, and she wouldn't be seeing it anyway. It might as well have been one that I never had glimpsed before. I made her uncomfortable with the book, but couldn't get her to put it back for another one, so I gave that up. I was keeping attuned to the time; I didn't want her to miss Arnold Greeley's broadcast, and I knew I couldn't trust her to turn it on without prodding. She detested him. I don't hate him. I am interested in him and in what he's doing. She is pure animal; all reaction, no cerebration at all. Time is a problem with her. I have to keep track of it for her and then sometimes she won't acknowledge my signals. For me, of course, there is her now, and all other times. That is bothersome too. There is all other time, all equally true and clear and available to me, but as she moves farther and farther away from her past she loses events and names and dates. They aren't repressed; she simply can't find them, and we can't make contact. Then, often, so much of what she thinks she is remembering is wrong. She said, "I wish I could break through and see what's really in there, go exploring in my own mind, you know?" She doesn't remember saying it, but she did, when she was fifteen, and very intense, and rather intellectual for her age. I thought then, how marvelous it would be to be able to open to her, to be one with her, but I saw that I was wrong. Those few times when she has had a glimpse she has been terrified.

Too, she misinterprets. She digs out a piece of something, adds conscious judgment, the "logic" she has acquired, to color it wrong, and thinks she has the truth.

I was thinking along those lines, also keeping in mind that the news would be on shortly, checking the pages that she turned to confirm that I had them all already, feeling with her the heat of the water slowly cooling, smelling with her the scent of the bath oil, the fragrance of the soap, enjoying the feel of the fluffy cloth, comparing it to a cloth she'd had at three, remembering the smell of her mother leaning over her bed, keeping a check on the fire because she hadn't closed the screen, wondering what her father would have said about her not wanting a baby. . . . I was comparing the bathroom with other bathrooms, the ones she'd had in her first New York apartment, the outhouse at camp when she was eleven, the mauve-papered one in her mother's house. . . . Each one was there, could be entered and examined, cracks counted in the tile, and so on. None of this reached her, of course. She was a blank. Presently she left the tub and wrapped herself in a heavy robe and warm slippers and curled on the couch in the living room before the television.

She watched the screen, sipping a third drink. She was warm now and felt sleepy and comfortable. The war news, the President's latest message, a senator's caustic reply, weather, minor items. Then Arnold Greeley was there, handsome, serious, father to the world.

". . . to give in to such evil. Never has this great nation faced such internal unrest, such unwarranted castigation by its own citizens, such treasonous deeds and threats, such blatant propagandizing of its youth . . ."

Margaret stared at the screen and didn't notice when the newscast ended, when the string of commercials started and stopped, when the movie *Intermezzo* began. Somewhere about the middle of the movie, she jerked away and staggered up from the couch to turn off the set and go to bed. She switched off lights in the small house and closed the door of the brown and white room. The closet door was open and she saw her reflection there in a full-length mirror. She pulled off her robe slowly and stared at the person she saw across the room, thin, good legs, long hair that was darkening but had once been the color of pale honey, blue-green eyes. She groped for the light switch behind her, and only the dying fire lighted the room then. Still she stared at the image and very slowly she raised one hand to her breast, feeling her flesh, pinching the nipple until it responded. She stepped closer to the mirror and watched her other hand move. She wanted to close her eyes, wanted to stop, wanted to cry, and did none of those things. She was staring into the mirror, but to the side of it I could see the brown corduroy coat, could feel the texture, smell the man smell of it. Margaret cried out then and fell across the bed sobbing almost hysterically.

I felt only disgust for her. She hadn't finished it and now would be up for hours, restless, demanding, not allowing me to have that small bit of freedom that I felt was my due. And in the end she might even decide on sleeping pills. I tried to make her go back to the motions that would bring about orgasm and finally rest, but she twisted and squirmed and sobbed and refused to touch her own body again.

Chapter 2

She had a bad night and awakened sluggishly, hearing, but not recognizing the sound, a pounding on the back door of the small house. Harry Dyerman, the grocer's son, I tried to tell her, but the wall between us was never more solid than that morning. She yanked on her robe and ran her hand through her hair. It doesn't tangle when she sleeps. As long as it is, you'd think it would, but it doesn't.

Harry was sixteen, maybe, embarrassed and uncomfortable when she opened the door for him. He carried a large grocery bag and tried not to look at her. Margaret's feet were cold; she hadn't put on her slippers.

"Dad said that if you didn't need the stuff I should bring it back, and to give you this." Harry handed her an envelope.

Margaret started to put it in her pocket, turned, asking, "How much do I owe you?"

He looked stupidly at her and shook his head. Margaret realized that Josie must have paid weekly, or monthly, or something. She rubbed her eyes hard. She should say, I'm not Josephine Oliver, kid. She felt the envelope then as the silence grew, and she pulled out a sheet of notepaper wrapped around a check. The check was for $54.50, made out to Josie. She stared at it, feeling as stupid as the boy looked. The note: "Dear Miss Oliver, Here is the balance from the one hundred dollars you left me. I paid Alice 8.50 to clean, and took out the 37 you owed me. Leaving a balance of 54.50. I didn't know where you was or I'd of mailed it to you. Yours sincerely, Gus."

She started to slip the check in her pocket and jerked it out again. She couldn't keep Josie's check, or cash it. She held it out for Harry to take back, and he took a backward step. He was staring at her now.

"Tell ... tell Gus to keep it, to pay for the things I'll be getting while I'm here," she said.

Harry took the check, but still didn't leave. She waited. "Dad says do you want someone to come up and clean for you?"

Alice? Did Alice always come to clean? She'd know Josie by sight. ... I tried to reach Margaret again, but she was having none of me that morning. She said, "I guess so. ..."

"He'll send Mrs. Carmichael over tomorrow, or whenever you say."

"Alice?"

"She busted her leg ice skating last winter and she's staying with her daughter down in Jersey somewheres now."

After Harry left, Margaret put on coffee and found her slippers. I almost felt sorry for her. She wasn't able to cope at all, and there was a call coming up, and the coffee would boil over, and the stupid boy had forgotten the furnace and would be back. ...

She tried to ignore the phone when it rang, but it went on and on and finally she answered it.

"Miss Oliver, this is Horace Bok. May I come over to see you this morning? I'm over at Baiting Hollow . . ."

Margaret said, "I'm sorry, you have the wrong number."

"Please, Miss Oliver. I know you're back! Don't hang up. Just hear me out. Please!"

"Mr. Bok," she said desperately, "I just got here, I haven't even unpacked yet . . ."

"Dr. Bok," his voice said softly, almost whispering. Then accusingly, "You've forgotten all about it, haven't you? You wrote to me that when you came back I could look over the material, and you've forgotten. . . ."

"Mis . . . Dr. Bok, I have to go. Coffee is boiling over. Good-bye."

She mopped up the coffee, then poured herself a cup and sipped it as she began to go through the bag of groceries. Strawberries, cream, cheese, lettuce, ham slices, scallions. . . . Dyerman had been thorough. There was even a loaf of raisin bread. She wrinkled her nose. Raisin bread? I was wondering how Bok had learned that she was there in the house. Through Dyerman or the agent who had arranged for the electricity to be turned on, probably. Horace Bok. I never had heard his name before. What material did he want from Josie? Margaret wasn't even curious about it yet. She was headachy and mildly hungover, and trying hard to remember the dream she'd been having when the pounding on the door interrupted her sleep.

It was a simpleminded dream, but she would make a big to-do about it if she recalled. I had heard the jeep turn from the road into the drive, and I had told myself a story about it: Bennett, in uniform, delivering a message to Garcia by jeep, being shot at by gorillas with poison darts, with Greeley in the background—Greeley being Garcia in this case—afraid Margaret would distract Bennett's attention long enough to permit one of the darts to get past his flying hands that kept knocking them aside before they hit him. One of the gorillas had started to beat on a hollow log, rotted at both ends, I had added maliciously, and that had taken care of the boy's pounding on the door.

She tried to recapture the content, and I kept pushing it out of her reach, until she gave up and sliced a piece of raisin bread and spread it with the sweet butter that Dyerman had sent. What material does Bok want? I kept pushing that up for her to seize on, but she sidestepped again and again. I looked over the rooms and decided to make her go through the desk drawers. She was reluctant. She's a rather decent sort, doesn't pry into other people's mail, and like that, but I made her anxious about Bok, enough so that she decided to try to find out who he was at least.

She found Josie's correspondence with him. Josie hadn't thought enough of it to take it with her when she left apparently. Also, Josie had not met Bok personally. Margaret sighed in relief. I did too. She had accepted the role of Josie. Things had gone far enough along already that to deny it meant far more explanation than simply to accept it for now.

There was Bok's initial note, with a letter of introduction from Dr. Luther Monroe, who addressed Josie as, my dear Josie, and who vouched for Bok's authenticity. He was a doctor of philosophy at Columbia, well known to

Luther Monroe, respected, etc., etc. Margaret's eyebrows
peaked and she went through the rest of the correspondence quickly. Bok wanted to look over the notes and
notebooks of Paul Tyson, which he understood were in
Josie's keeping. Josie had agreed that he might do that
when she returned.

Paul Tyson. The brown and white room was Paul's
room, Paul's books, his desk ... I looked at it again and
knew that Paul Tyson was the owner of the room, of the
brown corduroy coat. . . .

Margaret put down the letters and drummed her fingers
on the desk thoughtfully. Of course, she'd have to tell Bok
that he'd mistaken her for Bennett's aunt, but then he'd
tell Dyerman, or the agent, and someone would come to
find out just who was in Josie's house, and she really
couldn't prove a thing except that she was Margaret Oliver
and had the keys to the place. She didn't even know how
to get in touch with Bennett until he called her back.

On the other hand, she could admit Bok and let him see
the material. Josie had told him he could. He'd expect her
to know where it was, something about it. The letters
implied that Josie knew all about it, whatever it was.
Notes and notebooks. She wandered into Paul's room and
stared at the desk, bare and clean, with only the jug of
pens to indicate that it had been used in the past. The
drawers held supplies: paper, erasers, two unused typewriter ribbons, rulers, a compass, graph paper. . . . She closed
the drawers and looked over the bookshelves. All bound
books. Nothing in the closet, just his clothes, shoes,
sweaters, shirts. The dresser drawers held personal belongings, brushes, cuff links, underwear, socks. That settled
that. Josie must have whatever material Bok wanted to see.

When he called back she'd tell him it was not available at that time. It was in London.

Anyway she couldn't let him come out to the house. No matter what he said, or Josie had said to him. She stopped in the doorway at the thought and remembered the night before.

She had lain across the bed sobbing, frustrated, ashamed. She had a dozen books in the trunk of the car, all concerned with sex customs, practices, needs, perversions. At one time she had thought she would leave them on the coffee table, one at a time, for Bennett to find and, hopefully, read. But that had seemed so much like pleading for something else, more, different. He would have been surprised and shocked. He was very careful, making absolutely certain that she achieved orgasm, most of the time anyway, so what more could there be?

I had gone into the whole thing, but she had stopped herself from thinking about Tim, about Frank, and finally Bennett and marriage. She had refused Tim and Frank, each time at the point where it was really impossible to refuse, but she had, and then had lain awake writhing, wanting to be able to redo it all. Would it have been the same? She couldn't bear to think about it. She had sat up shivering in Paul's bed, staring at the embers of the fire. The first man, she promised. . . . She was always making promises to herself, wording them just so, listening to her silent voice mouthing them. The first man who is over twenty-five, she corrected, and added hastily, and has clean fingernails, and doesn't have thick lips. . . . She started over then: the first eligible man who doesn't have a marriage that might be endangered, who is over twenty-five, and under sixty, who has clean hands and doesn't have moist thick lips. ... She got up and made another drink, a strong one, and took it back to bed with her, and then sat huddled in the blanket watching the dying embers of the fire, sipping now and then, not thinking at all.

Standing in the doorway, she knew that she didn't dare let Dr. Horace Bok intrude on her that day. That was her problem. I was thinking of something entirely different. The bathroom that connected the two bedrooms in the house shared a wall with the two bedroom closets. Paul's closet, Josie's on the other side, the bathroom. I examined the wall again, seeing the smooth plaster painted white, with molding in his room, not in hers. Eight feet from the closet doors to the bathroom door ... bathroom three feet back closet two feet, room for pipes and two or three feet unaccounted for.

Margaret was reckoned to be intelligent. She had gone to college, had got her B.A. and worked, very successfully, as a personnel director for a computer firm. She understood some science, some math, some literature, and had enough sense to fake what she didn't know. Until she could find out, if that's what was called for, anyway. But aside from formal education, she was called intuitive, so I knew that I got through to her more often than I gave either of us credit for. I wanted to get through to her then, make her find the space between the bathroom and the closets and find the notes and notebooks that I knew had to be there. She was still grappling with the problem of her sexuality and the senseless promise she had made herself. She is very stubborn, and has what is almost a superstitious dread of breaking promises, even those given to herself, or perhaps especially those.

I couldn't break through. She had a headache, and those

maddening thoughts that revolved constantly, and there was no way I could get through to her. I considered. If she would only take a nap, it would be simple, but she was too agitated to think of that. I retreated and thought about it, and looked over the whole scene. I could see her swimming, see her on the phone again, see her poring over the notebooks. . . . Well, I'd get there somehow, but the how wasn't in the picture I got then. It's rather like a free-floating, four-dimensional filing system in no particular chronological order. I tried again, backtracking her steps, and yes, she did take a nap, and I did tell her how to find them. . . .

Margaret swam that morning, staying in the water only a few minutes; it was icy despite the hot sun. She showered and rubbed herself briskly, avoided the mirror, and pulled on her slacks and sweater, her own this time. A wind was rising, probably it would become quite cold before night. She had to get the furnace turned on. She started to phone, decided against it, and instead went out to the car to unload the trunk. The books were in a large brown bag. She had brought them along to get rid of them. She didn't take any of them from the bag. The swim and the hot shower had relaxed her, and she was humming as she reentered the house. The phone shattered her serenity. With her hand on the receiver, she let it ring and ring. When it stopped, the silence of the house was oppressive.

She continued into the bedroom then and put the bag of books by the fireplace. Later she would burn them, one by one. She sat in the leather chair and looked out at the waves and the sun dancing on them and she realized that Josie must have left the papers in the house. Why take them and leave everything else that belonged to Paul? If they had been left, they had to be in a particular place where they would be safe, relatively safe. She felt drowsiness creeping over her, pleasantly heavy, warm, comfortable. I knew the phone would start again. There seemed to be less time in this deserted part of the world than there had been in the middle of Manhattan. I shoved a picture of the only possible space for such a hiding place before her eyes and she couldn't see it. I was intercepting everything I could before it came to her attention then: a slight cramp in her leg that was drawn up under her, a crick in her neck from the awkward position of her head, turned to follow the flight of a gull, a mild beginning of hunger. . . . She was aware only of comfort and warmth, and then nothing. I made it as simple as possible, the closet opening in the right side, shelves behind the opening, papers ... The telephone woke her up, and her foot was sound asleep so that she had to hobble and hop to answer the insistent ringing. I couldn't let her forget the dream. She picked up the pencil on the table by the phone, and keeping her attention away from her fingers, I made her write the word "closet."

"Hello, oh, Mr., I mean Gus."

"Harry says he forgot the furnace, Miss Oliver. He'll be back a bit later. I credited your account with the fifty-four dollars."

"Oh, thanks. That's fine."

He added that Mrs. Carmichael could come up to the house three days a week, if she was needed, and Margaret said one day would be fine, and they both hung up. Margaret started for the kitchen and I made her stumble and catch the table for support. Her hand fell on the paper with "closet" written on it, and she remembered.

After pushing all the clothes to one side and feeling up and down the wall for a door of some sort and not finding anything, Margaret was ready to believe that her dream had been less than prophetic. She went to Josie's side and did the same there and again found nothing. With a shrug she left the whole thing to make a sandwich and coffee. Gus had sent tomatoes, and as she sliced one and watched the juice drip along the cut, she remembered reading in a spy novel how the hero had found a hair crack using a foaming detergent that stayed in the line after being wiped carefully from the surface of the wall. She laughed at herself, but she called Gus back and ordered a foamy detergent in a spray can. She was amused by the problem then.

"It's out of my hands," she told herself cheerfully. "If I find the papers and stuff, I have to vamp Dr. Bok. If I don't find them, I'll simply shoo him out of the picture by telephone and that's that." She rehearsed vamp scenes in her mind as she cleared away her scraps from lunch. Gus had said Harry would be along about three, and it was one-thirty. She decided to take a walk along the beach and she was whistling through her teeth when she started.

The wind was getting stronger and cooler, and now clouds were forming in the north, a heavy black line of them, like a shade being drawn across the deep blue. A tug labored with a large ship in the distance, and gulls screamed at her and wheeled threateningly over her head. She laughed at them and threw rocks and watched the idiotic birds swoop for them. She found that she couldn't walk very far in either direction. To the west a heap of rocks and boulders extended into the water, and she regarded the mound speculatively. Another day she would

clamber over it and continue, but not then. She retraced
her steps, hitting the same spots in the sand, amused by
what looked like a single trail that simply ended ten feet
before the rock pile. Going east she was stopped by a wire
fence that also extended into the water. Wire cutters, she
thought, furious with anyone who would obstruct a beach.
The shade was a third of the way across the sky by then,
and the wind smelled of cold wet weather coming.

Harry returned a bit before three and he vanished into
the basement that was large enough only for the furnace
and hot water heater, emerging moments later. He ducked
his head and took the dollar she offered him, and left.
Margaret read the directions on the spray can, stood
weighing it in her hand, and, returned to the closet. It was
brightly lighted, a very nice closet, she said to herself
mockingly, hearing Bennett's voice. She shook the can
furiously and sprayed the foam on the wall, then gasped
and gagged as the vapor came back to hit her in the face.
Her eyes tearing, coughing, she staggered backward out of
the small space and held onto the door for a moment
trying to cough the stuff out of her throat. When she could
see again, she looked into the closet. The foam was gone,
but there, outlined in white that was vanishing as she
watched, was a four-foot-high rectangle. The door.

Margaret searched for a method to release the catch and
open the door for the next half hour. She couldn't find it.
When the foam evaporated she couldn't even find the
outline of it again. Baffled, she went over the entire closet,
feeling every inch of it. Then she did the same to the
closet on the other side. Nothing. Finally, acting on impulse, my impulse, she went into the bathroom and looked
for something there that would open it. A double basin

with a double medicine chest over it was on the same wall. Inside the medicine cabinets there were men's things: a shaving brush, razor blades, an empty can of shaving lather, toilet water, aspirins, Band-Aids. . . . She couldn't see the top of the cabinets; they were flush with the wall, with a chrome ledge extending half an inch. Her fingers came to within an inch from the ledge. I remembered Bennett's description of Josie: taller than you. . . . A button on top of the chrome ledge wouldn't be out of her reach. Margaret thought of it too, and pulled a chair into the bathroom, climbed on it, and found a small black button that she pushed. When she got back to the closet, the door was open.

The notes were there, notebooks, a box of letters, loose sheets of paper covered with figures and doodles. . . . Margaret sighed with satisfaction and pushed the door shut again. She had taken nothing out.

She went back to the kitchen and made coffee. Now what? She knew she couldn't permit anyone to see what Josie obviously prized highly enough to hide that well. Yet Josie had told Bok that he could go through the material. It was Josie's decision, not hers. She sat down, drumming her fingers on the table and reasoned it through. She had promised herself, she had to find out if sex was the same with any man. She knew she had to find out, and she knew she would not find out as Mrs. Bennett Oliver. But as Josie Oliver? Bok would never know. It wasn't quite the same as being unfaithful. It wasn't at all like taking a lover, or having an affair. It was something that she should have done years ago, long before marrying anyone. And as Josie Oliver she could do it. Besides, Josie had promised him. One time. She would let him in, arrange things, give him the stuff he wanted and make him promise to return it in two days. When he brought it back, she would be ready to leave, so he would have no excuse to linger or try to see her again. She'd go back to Manhattan that same day. It would be done, and she would know. She thought it through from every angle and could see no flaw in her reasoning. Bok would have clean hands, she told herself. A doctor of philosophy, he would have to have clean hands. She remembered the other conditions and decided to let them take care of themselves. If he was too old, or married to a jealous wife, or any of those things, she'd simply hand him the stuff and try again another time.

Chapter 3

I tried for an hour to make her understand that she had to get the notes and things out of the safe and at least read through some of them before Bok called again. At six the thought came to her from nowhere that she had to have an idea of what was in the notes, and that she couldn't very well open the safe and get them out in front of Bok. Sometimes it is not easy.

What if he doesn't call back? she asked herself. He will, she answered. She was sure he would. She carried the notebooks to the desk and arranged them on top of it, then thought better of it and took them instead to the living room and put them in a stack on an end table. They were black loose-leaf notebooks, bound in leather that creaked in her hands. Most of them were filled, pages of figures, page after page of densely written material. She went back to the closet; there were folders of yellow paper, rough notes probably, not yet ready for transfer to the notebooks. She took them also to the living room. Then she closed the safe and pushed the clothes back in place. She remembered the chair in the bathroom and returned it to the kitchen.

She prepared dinner for herself, broiled lamb chops, tomatoes, lettuce, strawberries. She was eating when Bok called again.

When she heard his voice she felt a lurch in her stomach, and her hand tightened on the receiver painfully.

"Dr. Bok, I'm sorry I was so abrupt earlier. I was tired."

"My dear Miss Oliver, please. It was rude of me to call before you had a chance to rest. Have you reconsidered? May I come around to see you?"

She took a deep breath and closed her eyes. "Yes," she said, almost whispering. "Tonight. Eight? Is that convenient?"

His voice was ecstatic. He was delighted. Could he bring her anything? She hung up, her eyes still closed, and found she had difficulty in swallowing. She returned to the kitchen, but she could eat no more.

What if he's fat? she heard a voice asking, mocking her. She amended her qualifications: over twenty-five, eligible, clean hands, no wet thick lips, not too fat. . . . It was almost six, she realized with a start. Two hours. She had to change, had to read through some of the letters. She didn't know what Josie and Paul Tyson were to each other, where Paul Tyson was, why his things were in Josie's house. . . .

She pulled on a black shirtwaist that could be buttoned to the throat, or left open practically to the navel, black velvet pants, satin slippers. She wound her hair on top of her head in a coil and held it there with a velvet ribbon and then she opened the safe once more and took the letters to Paul's leather chair and started to read them.

Many of them were undated, and those that had dates merely said the day of the week, and the month: "June 2, Mon." They had been stored in no particular order. Margaret picked up one of his, bold handwriting, no wasted motions, no frills or flourishes, almost too sparse, hard to read at first.

Josie, my dear, the cottage is lovely now with purple shadows in the corners, a tinge of blue in the light that is remaining. It is so very quiet. Soon I'll put on a record, but now, listening to silence, watching the shadows fill the house, I am loath to move. I walked for miles thinking, arriving at no conclusions; but aware that something was happening to the data, finally. Then I came back to the empty house and there was a pain that nothing would erase, a need so sharp and immediate overwhelmed me that everything else paled beside it. Come home soon, my dearest. . . .

Margaret let the sheet of paper fall from her fingers and watched it settle on the table. She stared at the other letters and shook her head. What was she doing? Josie trusted her, trusted Bennett's wife, and here she was. . . . She pushed the letters from her, put them on the table, and stood up. She buttoned her blouse to the throat and thrust her hands deep in her pockets and started to pace. Did she need an analyst after all?

She had heard his voice as she read. A deep, resonant voice, very quiet and calm, honest. Did Josie deserve such a man, such a love? Margaret stopped pacing before the

table that held the letters. She stared down at them and
slowly reached out for one of Josie's notes, distinctive with
her mixture of print and script. Undated, short.

*My darling, we're a smash! They love us in Philly, and
they'll love us in New York. I'm sending a case of cham-
pagne home and I'll be there tomorrow night. If there's no
flight, I'll fly without one! I love you, love you, love
you.*

Margaret returned it to the rest and withdrew another
of Josie's letters, a longer one this time.

*Darling, I don't think I can stand it. I can't work, can't
sleep, can't do anything but think of you, of us together. I
used to be so cool, able to withdraw from anything and
work, but today when I stood in front of the bare stage,
you were there. When I tried to make sketches, your face
kept appearing on the paper. Thin, tired face, and that
crazy mop of hair every which way from the wind, and
bones like razors. I can't get your eyes. How strange that
your eyes can't be reproduced at all. It's because of the
light in them, you know. So I made them blanks, like
Little Orphan Annie's eyes, and then I laughed and I was
laughing and crying and smearing everything with tears. I
could hear your voice telling me not to fight it, to go to it,
whatever it was, accept all of it, but I couldn't. I can't. I
can't accept this ache, the hot pain that melts me to
nothing with desire. . . .*

Margaret started to tremble; she was very pale. She
gathered the letters together carefully and put them back

in the safe. I was thinking about Tim, who had caused her
to ache with desire, and I was wondering if that was what
Josie had meant. I hadn't been involved then at all, but
had been very interested. I was still interested in the scene
and examined it again in every detail. Margaret shivered
and almost ran to the kitchen to make a drink. She was
thinking of Tim too. Not of him, but of the feeling she
had experienced. One of his hands inside her blouse, the
other under her skirt. The delicious fear that came over
her in waves. She was having trouble breathing, afraid he
would continue, afraid he would stop. His hand hot on her
belly, her pubic hair, twisting gently, then suddenly a
burning probe, a stab that panicked her. Running, sobbing, afraid, and the hours in bed tormented, aching. No
more. She couldn't remember what had become of Tim. I
could have told her if she could have listened to me, but
the wall was there. He had called the next day, and the
next, and every day for a week. He had come to the house
twice. She had pretended illness, shame and misery making
her hide from him. And when she was ready to stop
hiding, he was gone, in the army. He had come back
married. Finis.

Margaret clutched the glass of bourbon and water with
both hands and drank deeply. What was wrong with her?
She never had been like this before. The drink steadied her
and after a moment she opened her eyes and took a deep
breath. It was after seven. Bok was due soon.

She went to the living room and opened the notebook
on the top. Paul's writing was small here, and the pages
were filled from top to bottom, with little margin left.
Also, he had used a cryptic shorthand, with initials, partial
words, incompleted sentences. She had opened the book in

the middle, and she turned it to the first page. It was a continuation of one of the other notebooks. The first page was headed "J.W.D.-cont."

She turned the notebook over in her hands, examining the cover. Finally she found the initials: PT-4. He sounded like a navy boat. She got the notebooks in numerical order then and opened the first one. It started with what appeared to be a critique of Jung. It began: "Jung, Syn. (coll.)." Margaret tried to read further, but it was all like that, and the words blurred and ran together. Without a clue about the subject matter, the notes remained indecipherable as if written in Swahili.

The chimes on the door sounded, and she jumped, upsetting her glass.

Bok!

She brushed an ice cube from her legs and blotted the wet spot with Kleenex as she went to the door. She was holding the soggy Kleenex in her left hand and the doorknob in her right when she opened it and admitted Bok. He seized her hand with the Kleenex and squeezed it, wringing a few drops of ice water that ran up her hand and wrist when he impulsively raised her hand to his lips and kissed it fervently.

"Miss Oliver, my dear Miss Oliver, I can't tell you how happy you have made me. After so many years, to have you return and bring back the precious notebooks. When I called first, I was filled with dismay, and it was like seeing the last gate being closed in my face. I had been so hopeful, so confident that if I were but patient enough . . ."

I was studying him closely, but Margaret was putty in his hands. He had pushed against her, and somehow the

door was closed, his hand still held hers, and if he noticed
the wet Kleenex, he didn't seem to mind. His lips were not
thick, and he was not yet sixty. Stout, but not fat. He wore
no ring, and his hands were clean, pudgy but clean. A
faint gloss on his nails, in fact. I looked at him more
sharply, but his interest in Margaret seemed genuine
enough. I caught some of his bewilderment and confusion.
Whatever he had expected, it was not Margaret.

"Miss Oliver, I know this occasion must fill you with
pain, to have a stranger intrude on you here, in this house,
on your first trip back, with the express desire to look at
his notes. Please forgive me. I would not give you one
second's worth of pain, if I could avoid it. If there is
anything I can do to alleviate . . ."

Margaret pulled her hand free and backed several steps
into the living room. She had an insane desire to say: kiss
me and shut up. She didn't. "Your coat, Dr. Bok. I'll put it
in the closet. Please sit down. Would you like a drink?"

Suddenly his hands twitched convulsively. He had
looked past her, had seen the books on the table. He
started to leap toward them, restrained himself, but he
couldn't take his eyes from them.

"A drink! Yes, that would be nice. A drink."

Margaret took his coat, but at the doorway to the hall
closet she turned and looked back at him. He had gone to
the table, had lifted one of the notebooks and was
clutching it rapturously to his breast. She shrugged and
went to mix him a drink, and to bring a cloth to mop up
the puddle on the floor.

Margaret poured bourbon into two glasses, added a
splash of water to one and drank it down. She unbuttoned
the first three buttons of her blouse, and muttered softly,

"He'll do." Then she made two drinks and carried them to the living room. Putting hers down on the coffee table before the couch, she handed the other one to Bok and at the same time removed the notebook from his clutching hand. His eyes followed the book back to the table where it was replaced on top of the others. He watched her as she cleaned up the spilled drink and then sat down.

"Sit down, Dr. Bok." Margaret patted the couch beside her, and he sat down gingerly. "Tell me something about yourself. Why you need the notebooks, what you are doing. Are you married?"

"What? No, not now. But surely you remember from our last talk, eight years ago ..." She shook her head gently. "Ah, of course. You were in shock, weren't you? How stupid of me. You see, I had this idea that I could establish a Chair of Chronosophy. . . ." He stopped and ran a finger around his collar. The uncomfortable feeling that he radiated was back again. "You're not, ah, that is to say, you are ... I had a different picture of you."

"Oh? Tell me," Margaret said, leaning forward slightly, her eyes on his face.

Bok drank deeply and sat up straighter. "I thought, you seemed, that is ... Uh, I haven't been around theater people much. You're very young, aren't you, to have your reputation? As a designer," he added hastily.

Margaret laughed, to hide the tremor that had started in her. She held her glass tighter and drank half the contents. She said, "Dr. Bok, really. You're here five minutes and already talking about age. And you, you are about fifty?"

"Fifty-four," he said, staring at her hard. He drank deeply again and ice hit the side of the glass and made him look at it. It was empty.

"Another one, Dr. Bok," Margaret said, taking the glass from him. At the doorway she paused and said, "You might want to look over those notebooks, make certain they are what you are after."

Bok nodded and reached for them. Inside the kitchen Margaret put the glasses down and held onto the sink for a moment, her eyes shut hard. Then she straightened and made two more drinks. She drank part of her own, refilled it, and returned to the living room, smiling graciously.

"Are you satisfied with them, Dr. Bok?" Again she took the notebook from him and put it in place with the others.

He nodded, watching her.

"I'm terribly sorry if I seemed to be prying about your personal life. Asking if you were married was inexcusable of me." Margaret looked down at her glass and swirled the drink about in it.

"Not at all," he said. "It was just one of those things; she got tired and left." He smiled to show that it was really over and they both drank again.

Margaret moved closer to him. She almost fell on him.

"Uh, Miss Oliver, are you all right? I mean ..." Margaret smiled and he said, "I'll take good care of the notebooks, you can rest assured. And I won't be in your way at all, quiet as a mouse, you know. . . . She smiled more broadly and her hand reached out to cover his.

"I know you will," she said. "But don't call me Miss Oliver. Call me ..." I could see that she was going to blow the whole thing, and since she'd had enough alcohol by then not to be able to do much about it, I took over.

First, I made the arm supporting her relax so that she did fall over on him. I didn't let her drink spill. She giggled and let Bok straighten her up. He kept one arm around her shoulders, and she giggled again, and relaxed against him. There was something else there, something that hadn't been there before. I tried to figure out what it was, but couldn't. Bok was planning something, that was all I knew. Her seduction? Hardly. She had taken care of that just dandy. Then what? I decided to wait him out. Margaret was mumbling something against his chest and he was still trying to decide if he should or shouldn't. With her against him like that he couldn't be unaware of the fact that she was wearing no bra, and that her blouse was open practically to her belly.

He put down his glass and touched her neck tentatively, and when she didn't pull away, he let his hand slide down. Margaret was still holding her own glass and she lifted it to her lips and drained it, creating an awkward situation, with her arm crossing his, pressing his hand against her body. He removed his hand and took her glass and put it down by his own. His hand took up where it had left off.

"My dear Miss Oli . . ."

She shook her head, making the room spin with the motion. "Not Miss Ol . . ." I plucked it right out of her mind and she forgot what she had started to say.

Bok said soothingly, "Josie, dear, I'm afraid you are very drunk. I shall have to put you to bed, you know." She sighed and he started her to her feet, toward the bedroom. He headed straight for Josie's room, one hand around her shoulder, holding her up, the other still at her breast. She staggered and would have fallen, but he caught her, and when her legs buckled, he lifted her and carried her the last ten or fifteen feet.

He put her down on the bed and started to undress her, but Margaret sat straight up and with great efforts said, "I am very drunk, you know. But I can undress myself." She closed her eyes and lay down again and said, "Thank you."

"Yes, my dear, of course you can," Bok said. He was quite deft with zippers and hooks and things. As he worked he murmured, "Poor dear, you've been so lonesome, haven't you?"

"So lonesome," she agreed, not opening her eyes. She was starting to sober up just a little, just enough to know how far things had gone, just enough to wish lightning would hit the house.

"You are so lovely, Josie, my dear. I had no idea . . ."

She was Josie. It was all right because it was Josie. Margaret was going, going, gone. It was all Josie's doing, not hers. She sighed again and murmured, "Lovely Josie is a bitch."

Bok grunted in surprise and I could hear him moving about the bedroom. I heard a drawer open and close softly, the closet door opened without a click and then closed again. What was the man doing? Margaret was falling asleep. He came back to the bed and again his hand on her breast aroused her, not with desire, but simply with wakefulness, and she sat up again. "Dr. Bok," she said clearly, separating each syllable, "are you going to screw lovely Josie or not?"

The telephone rang. Without looking at Bok, Margaret climbed down from the bed and walked, naked, to answer it. She walked very straight, not quite upright, but very straight.

"Hello. Oh, Bennett. You're in some godawful place in the South, aren't you?"

"Margaret, are you all right?"

"Course I am. I am very drunk, but all right. You can't give me your telephone number now because I can't seem to see quite right."

"For God's sake, Margaret. What are you doing up there?"

"Celebrating. A return to the country. The ghost of things past. What are you doing down there?"

"Margaret, I'll call you in the morning. Get to bed, get a good night's sleep. Don't smoke in bed, darling. Will you remember? *Don't* Smoke In Bed!"

"Don't smoke in bed," she repeated obediently. It was a stupid conversation, she decided, and started to hang up.

"Margaret, listen carefully for a minute. Don't let anyone take anything from the house at all. Do you understand?"

"No," she said.

"Good God! Margaret, pay attention. Josie called me from Italy ..."

"She isn't in Italy."

"Yes, she is, and she called me. She tried to call you and got no answer. She says no one is to remove anything whatever from the house. Under no circumstances. Do you understand what I'm telling you?"

Margaret understood all at once and she started to shiver. Bok was coming up behind her, but I didn't nudge her or anything. This was all very interesting and curious. Margaret sensed him then and she said, "I have to go be sick now. Goodnight." She didn't wait for Bennett's answer, but hung up.

Bok wrapped his arms around her from behind. He was undressed also by then. "You're shivering," he said.

"I'm shivering," she agreed. She slipped down under his

arms and hurried to Josie's room. Bok was right after her. Margaret stepped into the bathroom and closed and locked the door. She could hear him breathing on the other side of it. "You'd better go now, Dr. Bok," she said after a moment.

"Go?" Silence. "Josie, my dear, come out. Please come out."

"Not tonight," Margaret said, her ear pressed against the door. He tried the handle. Silence again. Then the other handle from Paul's room turned quietly, but that door, too, was locked. Margaret stared at it and suddenly she realized what I had known all evening. Bok had been there before. He knew the rooms, knew about the connecting bath, knew which door had led to Josie's room. Margaret stiffened. She could hear him in Josie's room again, making putting-on-clothes sounds. She slipped into Paul's room and snatched her robe from a chair there and pulled it on. When Bok left Josie's room, Margaret was standing with his coat at the front door.

He hesitated. "Goodnight, Dr. Bok," Margaret said and handed him the coat. He glanced at the table, then at her, and finally accepted the coat.

"I'll be back tomorrow, about noon," he said.

Margaret said nothing. When he left, she made certain the door was bolted. Then she returned the notebooks to the safe, and for a long time she sat staring at nothing in particular.

Chapter 4

I had been going over the whole evening, adding details that Margaret had forgotten, or hadn't seen, and trying to puzzle out answers. Chronosophy? That's what he had said. Study of time? Paul had been interested in time, too, obviously. Many of the books on his shelves had to do with time, and all the notes that I had seen. But what was there to know? How to go about studying it? Margaret had to get the notes out again and read them. That was my next project.

She was huddled on the couch, miserable, trying to remain blank, but not able to. She could see herself naked on the bed, under Bok's hands, and she wanted to cry. Exposing herself to him on the couch. . . . What could he think of her? Not her, of Josie. She tried to draw herself into a smaller knot. She'd have to leave early in the morning, before he got here. She should pack now.

The phone jolted her. Bok? It's Bennet, you fool, I said. She paid no attention, but stared at the telephone, willing it to stop. I carefully formed a picture of Bennett and she

41

almost saw it, enough to make her lift the receiver. She could always hang up if it was Bok.

"Margaret! Are you there?"

"Bennett. Oh ..."

"Are you all right? I've been so worried about you."

"I'm fine now. I . . . I had a drink on an empty stomach I had forgotten to eat dinner. I'm fine now."

The anxiety faded from his voice, leaving it merely petulant. "You have no idea of how you frightened me, Margaret. Alone there, drinking, sick . . . I want you to go back to the apartment first thing in the morning. I don't like the idea of your being there all alone. I'll give Shirley a ring, have her come out to the apartment and keep you company. . . ."

Shirley! Margaret tightened her grip on the receiver. "Don't be ridiculous. I need a rest away from the city, and I'm getting it. I told you, I forgot dinner. I was out in the wind and swimming and walking and a drink hit me hard. That's all. I'm perfectly all right now. I don't want to stay with Shirley for the next two weeks."

"Margaret, will you please think of me for a change. I can't be of any use to Greeley if I have to be worrying about you all day and night. I don't think it's good for you to be alone. . . ."

"Bennett, shut up, will you?" Margaret heard his gasp, and she took a deep breath and tried to force a wisecracking sound into her voice. "You're like a mother hen with an errant chick. Tell me again what Josie said to you. I must have been down at the beach when she called."

"Yes, she said it rang and rang. I don't know what was on her mind. I told you what she said. No one is to be allowed to remove anything from the house. She wouldn't go into any details, but said you'd know what she was talking about. Do you?"

Margaret stared at the fireplace across the room. How had Josie known she would understand? The silence grew too long and Bennett was back, sounding anxious again. She said, "I was trying to think what she could mean. A man did call for an appointment for tomorrow. Horrace Bok. Do you know him?"

"Oh, him. He tried to get in to see me a couple of times. He's writing a book and wants some information that he thinks Josie has. Don't let him in."

"He said he's a philosophy teacher at Columbia," Margaret said, not quite inflecting it.

"He is. Perfectly respectable and all that. But what good would it do for him to see you?"

"All right," she said, and he seemed to accept that. She wrote down the number of the hotel. Bennett would be there until Monday.

She hung up and wandered into the kitchen. She was hungry and there was a fierce storm pounding the house. She wondered if she had closed the car windows, but didn't go out to check. Pitted on the outside, wet on the inside. Maybe before she was through with it, she would scrape a long strip of paint off from front to rear. . . . She checked the thought and grinned at herself.

She drank a glass of milk and had the berries that she hadn't been able to eat earlier. Then she brought in a few logs from the back porch and made a fire in Paul's room. She turned off the lights in the house and sat looking out the windows at the storm lashing the pine trees. She could hear the surf now, and the wind, and the trees scraping the house, and the rain pelting down. The fire cracked and popped and snapped in the lulls. Bok, she mused. What was she going to do about Bok?

He hadn't asked if he could return. He had stated it, he would be back around noon. And he had been there before. He had said he was glad she had brought the notes with her, not that she had opened the house so he could see them. He had known they weren't in the house. If he had searched, why hadn't he found the safe? The lock must operate on electricity, so it wouldn't have worked for him. She tried to picture him as a housebreaker and smiled faintly. How frightened he must have been. What was in the notes important enough for him to risk a breaking and entering charge? When he hadn't found the notes in any of the obvious places, he must have assumed that they had been taken out of the house and so had abandoned his search for them. But now he knew they were there, and he would be back. Would he expect her to permit him to finish what he had started with her?

That was over, she decided. Not even as Josie. She tried to recall what she had thought and felt earlier when she had let him undress her, had felt his hands traveling over her body. Not much, she admitted. And yet, lovers all over the world implied that there was so much more to it than she had been able to discover.

"Sex is a simple act," Bennett had said. "Like eating, it can be very artistic and leisurely, with many refinements, and leave you feeling wonderfully well, or it can be done hurriedly without paying much attention to the content, and still achieve a certain satisfaction." Margaret stirred in Paul's chair, remembering the scene vividly.

I remembered it even more vividly. She had been nervous. It was a few months before their marriage and she had decided that making him wait was foolish and unnecessary. They were sitting facing each other in her small apartment and Bennett was holding a snifter of brandy. He had bought the brandy and the glasses to hold it after finding that she knew nothing about such things.

They had been to a movie, had walked back to her apartment, and her feet still tingled with the cold. He always came in with her, to check the apartment he had said the first time, smiling. She hadn't believed him, but that's all he had done. Tonight she had taken his coat and put it away in the closet and invited him to sit down. Bennett didn't like petting, or necking. "If it isn't going to lead to anything more than that," he had said, "you shouldn't do it. Arousal without gratification is not good for anyone."

So she had said, "Bennett, kiss me," and he had. She had kissed him back and finally he had put her down in the chair, had gone to pour the brandy, and was now lecturing her on sex.

"I know you're a virgin," he said. She blushed and he smiled at her. "I am very glad about that, Margaret. I've thought and thought about how it should be the first time, how not to frighten you, or hurt you, to try to give you pleasure the very first time so that you will grow to enjoy sexual intercourse."

Margaret pulled herself from Paul's chair and yanked the drapes over the windows hard. She turned on the light, blinking. Well, he had carried out his carefully laid plans, and then had spoiled everything by not having the self-control that he had credited himself with. When he asked if she wanted him to finish her with his hands, she had been revolted and disgusted. "You will learn, be as eager as I am," he had said. The room was too dark to see if he was smiling, or had his eyes closed half asleep, or anything else. Certainly he couldn't see the tears on her cheeks, and he made no motion to touch her then.

After that he was very methodical with her, never entering her until she was already on the point of orgasm, or hardly ever. She had grown to hate his wet kisses, and she could time exactly how long he would linger over her lips, how long with each nipple, exactly when his hands would start to slide over her body, down her thighs. . . . Now and then there was what he smilingly called a quickie, because he had so much stronger libido than she. It was either that, or he would have to resort to someone else for the satisfaction he required.

"My God," Margaret said to the sputtering fire, "seven years of that! What have I been thinking of?"

She shook the fire and added two of the sex books and the last log and told it when it started to blaze, "I hate him quite thoroughly, you know."

I wished she'd get off this kick and get out the notebooks, but she kept on staring at the fire as if she had just made a big discovery. She had hated him ever since that first night in her apartment, and she had even admitted it to herself a couple of years later, so why make a big thing out of it now? Possibly she had forgotten that she had made this decision. I looked around and saw that she had, completely. But she was thinking again. If she could be certain that sex was that simple act, that simple gratification that Benntet said it was, then it didn't matter whether or not she hated him. Everything else was bearable in their lives. And if that would be the same with any man, then she'd be better off if she didn't tilt the whole works. That's what she had to find out.

How? The only thing she had gained from the farce with Bok was the knowledge that she couldn't do it like that, not with just anyone who happened along. She thought of the many acquaintances who shared Bennett's business world: Forrest, Dwight, Eddie. . . . That was pointless. Same man with different names, they were all Bennett. People she had known before Bennett: Murray, Les, Cal. . . . That was just as bad. They had gone their ways, were out of sight now, forgotten. And weren't they also like Bennett? But who wasn't like him? Jason wasn't; he was a queer. She lighted a cigarette angrily. It was ridiculous that a woman of twenty-eight couldn't come up with a single man that she thought she might enjoy going to bed with. Hal ... he might do. Notorious reputation, married several times, single at present, but ... If he was all that good, why didn't any of his marriages last? He couldn't be very sure of himself, or he wouldn't have to keep trying someone new, and for her purposes, she knew she needed someone who was certain of himself, not another soul as uncertain as she was.

The fire was going to die, and she should either get another log or else go to bed, she thought, and this was another problem all at once. Nothing was simple any more. Finally, she went to the stoop and brought in another log; she knew she wouldn't sleep for hours.

The trouble was that she didn't believe in immortal love between man and woman, she admitted when the new log started to blaze. She glanced through an illustrated how-to manual, then tossed it in. She had heard enough women talk about great love, and had seen the love shatter and two empty people go separate ways. She didn't believe in the fiction she had read, and besides, if it really was a great love, the heroine, or the hero, died before the real test ever came, the test of mundane daily life together. No real love, no matter how sparkling in the beginning, survived that test, she was certain.

At some point love died and habit took over. It was easier to make love with the person who was available than it would be to go out to find someone else. And there was less danger of being rejected. Habit and complacency and laziness. The touchstones of marriage.

Had the affair of Josie and Paul withered under the onslaught of this deadly trio? Had she left him, taking all her belongings with her, driving away never to return? And he, alone with the purple shadows, had he simply walked away from everything? Margaret opened the safe and took out the letters once more, settling herself in Paul's chair, and she started to read them all.

There were a lot of them. Josie had been back and forth between the cottage and the city several times each month, and to California, and even to England twice. The letters spanned several years, three at least. It was hard to be certain because they weren't dated with the year. Margaret forgot her drink on the table next to the chair. She let her cigarette burn itself out and forgot to light anoher one. The fire burned brightly, then faintly, then died, and she didn't notice. Once she found that she was weeping softly, but she wiped absently at the tears and forgot them.

I was storing the contents, making order out of them, learning Josie and Paul through their words. I kept getting hints of something that was staggering in its implications, but only hints. One of Paul's letters said: "... such perfect union of two disparate beings, such a wholeness that never existed before. I felt your joy, your excitement. First just a brush as if with nothing more than a powerful suggestion that this is what you must be feeling, then stronger and stronger, until no longer was it 'as if,' it was what you felt. Tomorrow. I say it over and over. Tomorrow she will be home again. And even knowing that tomorrow is not now, I search and try to find you here. . . ."

The storm had ended and Margaret was falling asleep in the chair. Her fingers were holding the last letter she had picked up, but limply. I let her go. Searching? How? For what? I tried to look farther than I had even seen before: Margaret bathing, Bok, Bennett in the living room, Margaret running on the beach. I was spiraling, in larger and larger circles, searching as I never had searched, for what I didn't know. Finding areas of blankness, areas of childhood, areas of now, of yesterday, of tomorrow ... grayness, reeling back from nothingness, drawn again to it.

Everything gone. Solid gray, no boundaries, no horizon, no up or down. Grayness that was either infinitely far away, or else so tight against me that it smothered me. Grayness that held nothing. Or everything.

A touch. Recoil. No way out now. Alone, lost. Who was I, or what? A voice, not from outside, deep within, on, through. Not like any voice ever has been. "Don't run away. Don't be afraid."

Margaret, touching the strangeness, awakened, screaming softly in fear. A nightmare. She shivered violently but couldn't shake away the echoes of the nightmare. She felt suddenly that someone was in the house with her, someone watching her, ready to reach out for her. She was afraid to move, and strained to listen, trying to hear if there was anyone in the living room. Bok? Had he come back, entered the house? There was no sound, but the feeling of not being alone grew stronger. I tried to hear someone else, too, and failed. If there had been someone else in the house, I would have known it. I would have. I was afraid with her. Ghost stories stirred in her memory; childhood terrors walked again; stories of stranglers, of mad escapees, of spies and hostages, teen-aged monsters. . . .

She had to stir, had to make sure no one had come in. She was shivering so hard that she could hardly move from the chair. Her hand couldn't hold the poker the first time she tried to lift it. I was starting to recover by then; whatever it had been, there was no threat now. I had left her, permitted the nameless terrors to invade her as she slept, and now she was still feeling the effects. As I took over again, she became calmer, and could even stare at the poker with a grim smile. She checked the house, and, of course, it was empty and secure with the bolts on the doors properly in place and the windows all tight and not tampered with.

She returned to Paul's room and picked up the letters that had fallen to the floor and put them all away. When she turned off the light, the thin, dim light of early dawn filled the room. She dropped the poker and fell onto the bed and was asleep almost instantly.

What had happened? I didn't know. I had come across areas of blankness before, but they simply weren't filled in yet, or had been skipped somehow. This grayness was not like that. It existed and inside it there was no outside, nothing else, and it had drawn me deeper and deeper, or farther, or in a different direction altogether. Margaret?

What would have happened to her if I had been absorbed by the grayness, the nothingness? Would she have sat shivering in the chair until someone came in to find her?

And whose voice was it that had led me from the nothingness, led me back to Margaret and then left again? Whose? How?

Margaret had dreams until she was awakened by Bok's insistent hammering on the kitchen door. He must have thought she was in Josie's room, for he alternated pounding on the door with tapping on Josie's windows, then returning to the door again. Margaret finally stirred and roused enough to go to the door and call through it for him to go away and leave her alone. She turned to go back to the bedroom.

"Josie! Come back and listen to me a minute."

She stopped, but didn't return to the door. "I'm not awake yet," she said irritably. "Go away."

"Josie, I'm putting a few things in the apartment over the garage. I meant what I said last night. I promise I won't disturb you at all. I'll do my work out there. It'll take me an hour to get moved in, and by then you'll be awake and we can talk."

Margaret held her head with both hands hard. She said deliberately, "If you don't go away right now, I'll call the police."

"I don't think so, my dear." I pictured him glancing behind his shoulder in the brief pause before he continued. "You see, Josie, I know all about that last month. I know what you did, how Paul died, everything. I don't think you want the police out here any more than I do right now. I'll be back in an hour, my dear."

Margaret swayed. Paul dead! It didn't mean anything to

her. It couldn't. She had never heard of him until the day before, had no idea of what he looked like, who he was, what he was. But she felt bereaved and wanted to weep for him, for Josie. For herself.

She had to get out of the house, back to the apartment. Bok wouldn't leave her alone now, regardless of what she told him. He wouldn't go away, and she couldn't call the police. What if he did accuse Josie of . . . murder? Was he accusing Josie of murder? Margaret's head was pounding abominably by then; she put on coffee and, while it was perking, she got dressed. She had to think before Bok came back. She would call the electric company and tell them to turn off the power, and she would wait until they did that and then leave. Bok wouldn't be able to get inside the safe with the current off. He would think she had the notes and notebooks with her again. If he followed her into the city, she would simply keep driving until she lost him and then go home. Let him check the hotels for the next week or two, and the airport and train stations. She decided to call the company immediately, and I stopped her.

I thought Shirley at her intensely and she got the image. Bennett would think she needed someone to stay with her, and that would mean Shirley. Shirley was one of his Boston cousins; his parents had come from Boston and there were fourteen cousins from his mother's side of the family. All detestable, and worst of the lot was Shirley. Margaret stopped and forced herself to rephrase the statement. They were not detestable, she simply didn't like them, and they didn't like her. Bennett had married down in their opinion and they didn't hide that fact from her. But they were polite to an extreme, and Shirley wanted ever so much to help her, poor dear. "Darling, you don't open white wine before it is brought to the table, only red wine." Or, "Dear, you really must learn to use *Who's Who* before your guests arrive. Not to know that Dr. Baldwin was formerly the president of Merchants Bank was inexcusable. . . ."

Bok would be easier to take than Shirley. And, after all, what difference would it make to her if he sat in the garage apartment and read Paul's notebooks? He seemed to understand without her telling him that he couldn't take them away with him. All he wanted to do was read them, copy parts, probably, and then go on his way. Josie had said he could do that.

Margaret had coffee and forgot about calling the electric company. She was jumpy and on edge, but when Bok returned, she allowed him to enter, and without referring to the scene of an hour earlier, she said, "I put the things in the living room. You may take one of them at a time to the apartment, and if you tear anything out, or deface them in any way . . ."

He looked so shocked at the idea that she abandoned that line. "I'll give them to you as you need them. When you return one, I'll give you another one until you are finished. How long do you think you will need?"

Bok was all business that afternoon. If he remembered the night before he gave no indication of it. His face was shiny with the exertion of getting his equipment into the apartment, and there was a smudge on his shirt front. He said, "I'll need to read them all thoroughly, and then decide. I'd estimate two days for the initial reading . . . another two or three to copy material. . . . Can you allow me a week, my dear?"

It was both a question and a demand. Margaret didn't reply. She turned and went to the living room and came back with the first book. It was initialed PT-1

After he left, Margaret was furious with herself. What in the world was so doing? She was frightened that she had let that man, a stranger, take one of Paul's notebooks out of the house, that she hadn't called his bluff and forced him to leave, that she hadn't, as a last resort, gone back home and refused to admit Shirley, or anyone else Bennett might send to guard her. She felt very tired and hopeless about the whole affair.

I knew what I was doing, though. Bok knew what it was all about, and I wanted to know too. So, if from time to time Margaret found herself doing things she didn't want to do, and regretted doing afterward, that was the price we had to pay for information. I would continue to try to shield her from things she was better off not knowing, and try to inform her of those things that she should know. I would guard her sleep and watch her absentminded moments for her and do all the things that I accepted as my responsibility, but I would not let her leave the cottage, I had weapons that I had never dreamed of using on her, and I would pull them all out if I had to. I had to find out about that gray nothingness. I had to find out whose voice it was that had led me out of it, back to her, and how and why.

Chapter 5

Margaret walked on the beach until she came to the pile of rocks and boulders, and then sat down in the sunshine with the brisk wind in her face. She would be sunburned, she thought, but didn't move. She heard the jeep when Harry delivered her groceries, and then silence returned and gradually she became calm enough to try again to think about what she was doing, what she could do. She felt that she was being pushed one way and then another, and apparently she was helpless to resist. She dismissed Bok from her mind and concentrated on her problems with Bennett, but her mind refused to remain fixed. Bennett didn't solidify in her thoughts. Instead of thinking about the very difficult decisions that she couldn't dodge forever, she found that she was wondering why he had married her in the first place.

His family was so very proper, Bostonians for three centuries with never a mistake in the family. Until Josie. Really an afterthought, sister to Bennett's father, born when Bennett was three years old, she had been wild from birth on, or so he said. A sport, he had said, and at the time Margaret had thought he meant something else, but, no, he had meant a biological sport.

Margaret shook her head and forced her mind back to Bennett, away from Josie and the family. She couldn't keep him in focus. Because she never had understood him? Not exactly, she said to herself. Not that. Because she never did know why he wanted to marry her. That was the crux. If she knew that, it might be easier to know what to do now. And it would be easier to know what to do about her pills. For almost five years she had not used birth control, and nothing happened. Then she had decided that she didn't want a child, and she had got the pills, without telling Bennett. She threw a stone into the water, then another, and another. She threw them hard. So, she would tell him about the pills. Tell him that she absolutely refused to have his child. Tell him no more quickies. . . . She felt her muscle pull too hard and she dropped her arm to her side and sat rubbing it. How could she say that to him?

It was getting late; she had to go back, put away her groceries, bathe, and then what? Dinner, she thought with an effort. Everything required great effort these days.

She found Bok in Paul's room, seated at Paul's desk, with three of Paul's books open before him. He looked harassed.

"Josie, my dear, can you decipher this section of the notebook for me? I can't find any source . . ."

"Dr. Bok, how did you get in? What are you doing?"

"Damn it, Josie . . . Miss Oliver, you left the door open. I saw the boy enter, so I did too. Look, Josie . . . I may call you Josie, mayn't I? Can't we call a truce? I apologized for my very rude behavior, and you have been exceedingly kind to me. I appreciate it more than I can tell you. I know you want me to finish and leave you alone, and if you will help me, I will be much faster. You are familiar with his writing, you know his sources, his experiments. ... Look here ..." He held the notebook open, advancing toward her with it, pleading on his face.

Margaret drew back and shook her head. "I can't," she said vehemently, staring at the open notebook that was gibberish to her. "Leave me alone, Dr. Bok. I can't help you."

Bok looked startled by her reaction. He stopped half-way across the room and studied her intently. A strange look crossed his face, he became at once secretive and knowing, and excited. "Of course," he whispered. "Of course!"

Margaret looked up from the notebook in his hand to his face. "What do you mean, of course?"

"You helped him from the start, didn't you? When he uses 'O,' he refers to you, doesn't he? You're the source!" He snapped the notebook shut and beamed. "What a relief! I won't have to try to decipher his notes, after all. You can describe the experiments, the procedures, the safeguards. You know that I talked to him by phone twice, don't you? He told me then that it was exceedingly dangerous, and then his unfortunate ... However, you can fill in this whole area for me, can't you? Won't you?"

Margaret took another step backward, feeling for the wall behind her. She had to get rid of him. Everything he said was a threat; when he asked a question, it was a demand. She was trapped by her own inability to tell him the simple truth. He wouldn't believe her now, she thought, and didn't know that it was my thought handed over on a platter for her to seize. She would have to plead ignorance and let him make of it what he would.

"I can't help you," she said deliberately, her voice deceptively calm, too well controlled. "I don't know a thing about any of it. ..."

"You're ly ..." Bok stopped and examined her more closely, bewilderment and cunning passing over his face quickly, leaving it a blank again. "You have amnesia for that period, is that it? How strange. There's no reason for that. ..." He stared at her thoughtfully, but wasn't really looking at her then. He believed her at least, believed that she really didn't know anything about it. I could see when the new idea hit him, the lift to his sagging shoulders, the purpose that firmed him all over. He bowed to Margaret slightly and said, "Thank you, my dear. Thank you." He sidestepped her and left Paul's room, and in a few seconds the kitchen door closed and he was out of the house. I listened to him cross the yard, and mount the stairs to the garage apartment and open and close that door also. Margaret heard none of that. She was shaking. She wanted to go home, away from Bok and his mysteries, away from the house on the sea, away from that room. . . . She had wanted to say to him, "I'm not Josephine Oliver. I don't know anything about any of this." She had tried to say the words and only a silence had come of it. She was afraid she was going mad.

I tried to soothe her with images of the ocean in the late afternoon, with the memory of the sun glinting on water that looked like silver flowing on the sand. She rejected everything I offered up, and I knew she was determined to leave. I showed her a still picture of herself in a smashed automobile, obviously dead, three other cars wrecked in a pile that exploded into flame abruptly, shattering the stillness of the scene. She staggered and leaned against the wall. I took away the memory of the illusory scene and left only the "hunch" against driving again soon. Listlessly she left Paul's room and checked the bolt on the front door of the house, then went to the kitchen door to lock and bolt it. When she looked outside, she saw the car where she had left it and she stared at it for several moments, puzzled by her strong feeling about not wanting to drive. She had been a good driver for over ten years, had never felt like that before. She shrugged and went to draw her bath.

I was biding my time until she fell asleep that night, not impatiently, of course, just with awareness that I shouldn't leave her alone while she was up and awake. That could be dangerous. Early in the evening she decided to take sleeping pills, and nothing I could do dissuaded her. I tried to make her fall asleep on the couch, and she dozed again and again; the swirling thoughts about Bennett and Shirley and Arnold and Bok kept jerking her wide awake, and finally she made cocoa and got out the pills. It was only ten or so, extremely early for her. I made her drop the first two pills she shook from the bottle; she got out two more and swallowed them quickly. I could have stopped her, there are ways, but I decided that that wasn't the time to make her feel any more insecure than she was already. She had been pushed around quite a bit during those couple of days. So I felt the curtain being drawn over both of us and there was little I could do about it.

The sound of Bok's car leaving woke her up. She felt terrible, as she always did when she took pills. Coffee helped a little, but she couldn't face breakfast. The sun

was bright and it seemed that spring was advancing fast
now after the hard rain two nights ago. She opened the
back door to look out, and there was the Sunday *Times* on
her porch. She grinned. Sunday, by God! Another week.
She'd have to remember to tip Gus generously; he was
taking very good care of her. She brought the paper inside
with her and closed the door again. The sun's brilliance
was deceptive, the morning was quite chilly. Probably it
would warm up later and she would take a long walk,
exhaust herself thoroughly with outdoor exercise so that
she would be ready for bed and sleep without pills. Her
head ached, and it seemed to her that she had been living
with a headache for a long time. Maybe she had a brain
tumor, she thought, with a thrill of pleasurable fear. That
might account for everything that seemed wrong with her.
She sat down with the paper and another cup of coffee,
only to find that she wasn't reading it at all. She was
flicking pages rapidly, not catching more than a headline
here and there when the name of Arnold Greeley seemed
to leap from the page and strike her eyes.

*Arnold Greeley last night, in a strong antiadministration
attack, promised that his office would disclose within a
week the names of those he accuses of participating in the
riot planning of last summer, and he linked them, by
innuendo, to the State Department ...*

Margaret read it thoroughly and then put the paper
down and stared at it. What was he trying to do? He must
be crazy, she decided. She picked up the paper again and
read the commentary that accompanied the news story.

The All American Party is lashing out with renewed intensity against every institution of government, making accusations by the score that everyone knows can never be proven, if simply because of the numbers involved. Greeley is mastering the TV technique, however, and he puts on a good show, and generally he has his audience standing up with ovations for him time and time again. All he can hope for, as he well knows, is to create a schism in the two major parties and wield a power bloc that will make demands and have enough votes on hand to reward whoever promises to meet those demands. ...

She shuddered and turned to the entertainment section.

Bok returned with someone else while Margaret was making her bed. She had dressed in a warm sweater and wool pants, and heavy walking shoes. I couldn't hear what Bok and his companion said, but I caught their voices, and then two pairs of treads on the steps, the knock at the back door and again a murmur of their voices. Margaret was startled to see the second man with Bok. She didn't invite them in.

"Miss Oliver, this is my assistant, Morris Stein. I decided, since I am intruding, that with an assistant the work will go much faster. I trust you have no objections."

Margaret glanced at the second man and then shrugged. He seemed to be a well-dressed student, slight, dark, rather good looking, if a bit dissipated. Probably worked too hard, slept too little. Probably indebted to Bok for something that he was required to repay. Bok, in comparison, appeared cheerful and very well fed. Stein smiled shyly at her, made a tentative movement with his hand, not knowing if she would shake hands with him or not, then stuck it in his pocket. Margaret felt ashamed of herself.

Probably he was very nice, worked after school, had a nice girl friend who was waiting patiently for him to finish school. . . . She smiled back at him and said to Bob, "I hope you don't work Mr. Stein too hard."

Later as she clambered over the boulders she remembered that she had not locked the house, but she didn't go back. What was the use? Bok had a key anyway. She had left the notebooks out on the desk in Paul's room, so if he did go into the house, he wouldn't be tempted to try to find the safe. She reached the top of the heap of rocks and sat down panting. After her breath got back to normal she had a cigarette and leaned back against a sunwarmed rock and watched clouds for a long time. It was peaceful and quiet again and the air was warmer than it had been the day before. She opened her sweater, feeling drowsy. I waited, then knew it was hopeless. Someone was coming.

She jerked when she heard the soft, shy voice of Morris Stein very close by. "Miss Oliver, may I sit down?"

She had closed her eyes, but now opened them to see the young man just coming over the top of the boulders. Angrily she said, "Why did you follow me?"

He looked hurt and distressed and started to back down the way he had come. "I didn't," he said. "I was with Dr. Bok until a few minutes ago. He decided I should start work early in the morning, so I came out for a walk. I'm sorry I bothered you."

Margaret sighed. "No, don't go. My fault. I'm getting a little paranoid about your Dr. Bok. I was certain he had sent you to spy on me. Sorry."

Stein ducked his head and sat down about five feet from

her. He was puffing slightly after the climb. "I started to just turn around and leave," he said, "when I saw that you were up here, but I thought that if you had heard me, you would really think I was spying on you. I stood there for almost a minute trying to decide if I should announce myself, or try to slip away again." He smiled at her and said, "I'm glad I spoke up."

Margaret turned from him abruptly. He was about twenty-two or three, and seemed much younger than that even. Looking out over the water she said, "Are you one of his students?"

"Oh, no. I studied with him two years ago. Just one term. I'm doing my doctorate work on my thesis. It's 'Perception Distortions in Various Psychological States.' I may change the title later, but that's what it is."

"You're a psychologist? Research, clinical, what?"

"I do some clinical work now, but I want research later, after I get my doctor's degree."

"Then you'll go into sales motivation research and become very rich, or into political actions research and become powerful. . . ."

"Oh, no! Nothing like that! I want, first, to find out how we see what we see, and why we see things differently. You don't see what I do, for example, even when we look at the same . . ." He cut it off brusquely and she heard his feet clattering on the rocks. "I'd better go back."

"Oh, sit down," Margaret said, and she looked at him then. "You are very angry with me, aren't you? To suspect you of wanting to make money, or attain power. Why, I should have known from the cut of your jacket, and the shine on your shoes, and the crease in your slacks that you were above such worldly desires, shouldn't I?"

He blushed, then grinned at her. He sat down again. "Last year I did the hippie thing," he said. "But now, working in the hospital three afternoons a week ... The patients didn't seem to relate to a bearded, blue-jean-wearing information taker. That's about what it amounts to, you know. Besides, last fall my father died and left me some cash and I decided I liked clothes."

Margaret shook her head at him ruefully. "Stop. I don't want to pry into your life. I don't want any more details. I don't envy you the trip back and forth to the city, if that's what you plan to do."

"Oh, I'm off this week. And next. I work two weeks, off two." He skinned a flat rock that cut the water twice, then sank. He tried again. He wasn't very good. "I thought you were a lot older than you are."

"I keep hearing that," Margaret said, turning away again.

"It's unavoidable, I suppose. I mean, Tyson was in his fifties when he ... God damn it. I guess I really should leave now. You want a hand down first?"

Margaret stood up. "I'll manage," she said. "I'm going back too. The wind is cooler than it was a while ago." She started to slip and slide down the rounded rocks and his hand caught hers and held her steady until she was at the bottom. "Thanks," she said. He ducked his head and started to walk by her side, still holding her hand. She didn't pull loose.

Margaret was thinking of how long it had been since she had walked hand in hand with anyone, and couldn't remember the last time. His hand was warm, stronger than it appeared from his slight frame. He was wiry, she supposed. A lassitude was creeping through her that she didn't want to shake off. It was as if they were in another world, two young people walking along a beach holding hands, the warmth of his hand spreading through her gradually, making her forget the chill of the rising wind. He didn't squeeze her hand, or make any other movement with it, but held it securely, matter-of-factly, as if they had always walked that beach holding hands, and always would. Neither of them spoke. Margaret was watching her feet thrust before her, retreat, thrust again, particles of sand trailing. She was thinking of nothing, aware of her hand warm in his, of her feet moving through the sand, not much else.

I was being very careful not to let her share any of my suspicions about the young man and his motives. I didn't care what he was after if he kept her content for a time, but I knew he was after something and I was watching him closely. He was a curious combination of boyish innocence and man of the world self-assurance that was impossible to delineate precisely. The hand-holding business, for example, could have been simply a youthful, uninhibited, spontaneous gesture of admiration, or friendship, without any sexual overtones implicit in it. Or it could have been a deliberately deceptive gesture. ... Anyway, he had lied to her twice already and I was not going to let her know that, but I was going to watch him. He had lied about finding her on the rock pile accidentally. His stride hadn't been that of someone out taking a stroll. He had gone directly to her and then pulled the "sorry to intrude" routine. And he had lied about the clothes. They were good clothes and they were over six months' old. The suit he had worn when Bok introduced him was at least two years old, a fine worsted that would still be good looking in ten years.

Margaret wasn't aware of either of those facts. They came to the bank that led to the yard of Josie's house and he went up first and turned holding her hand for her to follow. At the top, in sight of the house and garage, she gently disengaged her hand and they walked side by side to her kitchen door.

"Do you want coffee, or a drink?" she asked.

Morris Stein shook his head. "Not now," he said. "I told Dr. Bok that I'd be back in time to go out to dinner with him. Later?"

She nodded and he turned and left.

Margaret mixed a weak drink and took it with her to the living room, where she swung her feet up on the couch and rested her head on the arm. The torpor that had overcome her deepened, and while she didn't actually sleep, she wasn't awake either. I left her like that.

I saw her and Morris and felt very pleased, then farther away I saw her in the ocean, swimming. . . . I went farther, finding the safe in Paul's closet, hurling a bookend at Bennett. . . . Farther, on a bicycle, hair streaming out behind her, dancing. It was the wrong way. Widening circles, but the center didn't change, always around her. How had I gone the other time? How else could I go?

Margaret tried to stir once and I returned quickly and soothed her. "Don't think, just don't think," I sent her, and knew that she had the impression of heavy legs and arms, of being pressed down by an intolerable weight. I removed it and let her feel buoyant, but relaxed. She became quiet again. I resumed the search. Still nothing. Why had it happened before?

She had been in Paul's room, immersed in Paul and Josie. . . . That must be the difference. I gave up and let her wake up thoroughly then. She felt very good, and hungry. After her dinner, I tried to make her return to Paul's room, but she was thinking of Morris Stein and to get through to her then would have shattered her serenity, so I waited and anticipated the visit with her.

She put on music and changed her clothes and brushed her hair, leaving it loose, held off her face with a ribbon. The record stopped and she put on another. It was nine-thirty. She made another weak drink and wandered through the house with it, then put it down on the table by Paul's chair. She decided that he wasn't coming and she sat down, to stare out at the moonlit world. She tried to hide her disappointment with relief at not having to make that decision when she obviously was in no condition to make it, but she couldn't. She wanted him to come back that night, had wanted to hold his hand again, to feel his presence near her. She hadn't really carried it past that, and it seemed such a simple thing, just her hand in his. She closed her eyes and while she was unmoving and unaware, I left again.

Everything was as it had been; she was consumed with desire for something that seemed unattainable; she was trying not to think, and succeeding to a certain extent; the influence of the room, of whatever it was that had influence in that room, was as it had been.

Not in the ever widening circles; they hadn't been the way. It had been another direction entirely. Up? What was up? I didn't know. Somewhere else in a place that was directionless. Margaret was all right, dozing on the chair, not smoking. I had to leave her. I had to be free of her. Straight through the circles, beyond all her time, blanks. Blank, but not the nothing that I had experienced. I don't know how long it was for Margaret, to me it seemed a moment. I heard from a distance a voice trying to rouse her.

"Josie, can you hear me?" Morris Stein, speaking rather softly, his hands gentle on her cheek, moving her head very slightly. Trying to wake her up? It didn't seem so. Very carefully he let her head go back on the chair again and he left her. I heard him say to Bok, "She's out. She's been drinking. Forget our plan and get out. I'll take care of her."

Bok's chuckle. "She gets pretty amorous when she's stewed. Don't forget to turn on the tape recorder. I'll wait up in the apartment." The door opening, closing, Bok's heavy tread ... Morris Stein returning, closing the door to Paul's room, kneeling by Margaret's side.

I was back all the way and curious. I let Margaret wake up and she sat up straight when she saw him. Newly awakened, she had no defenses that she could call up then; she was open to him if he wanted her, vulnerable, as she blinked in incomprehension.

"Josie, you looked so lovely just now, so sweet and young." Morris Stein took her hand and pressed it against his cheek. He was still on his knees and he pressed his head on her lap and slid his free arm around the small of her back. Margaret closed her eyes. The warmth of his cheek against her went through her pants, through her skin, deep inside where nerves responded; a wave of desire surged through her, tightening her stomach muscles, raced upward, making her diaphragm rigid so that she gasped for air. Her throat constricted and she had to swallow hard. It was so fast, over in an instant, but with a lingering aftereffect that left her feeling weak and helpless.

He released her hand and placed it on the arm of the chair. He unbuttoned her blouse and kissed the bare skin just above the waistband of her pants. She drew in a quick deep breath as a second wave started through her. His hand slipped behind her back and he undid the bra hooks and he slipped the blouse off her, then the bra. His hand on her back pressed her toward him and his lips passed lightly over the skin of her breasts. He was a real expert at work, this Morris Stein. When she shivered, he pulled her close to him, supporting her weight with both arms, and his left hand came just to the snap and zipper of her pants. He undid them and let his hand slide inside them and work them down her buttocks, out from under her. His hands caressed her as they passed under her, then under the backs of her legs, taking her pants down and off. Her hands tightened convulsively on the chair arms as suddenly the feeling of all-over desire became localized in a flash of fire which also spread and spread. As her stomach was exposed, he kissed it, her navel, the right groin, the top of her thigh. His cheek brushed the hair and she jerked, but he kissed the left thigh. She heard her low moan and felt her body moving now. Toward his hands and lips. He hadn't touched her nipples, any of the spots that Bennett worked over thoroughly; she had never known her skin could be so sensitized and responsive. He got the pants free of her feet, and flicked off her slippers. He kissed her feet, her insteps, the inside of her knees. He spread her legs slightly and ran his fingers up them, and again avoided the pubic area, but let his hands follow the lines of her groins to the hipbones, up her hips, her ribs ...

Margaret was moving rhythmically under his hands now, straining forward toward him, only half aware of when one of his hands left her as he started to take off his clothes. He was murmuring to her, softly, almost inaudibly, cutting off his own words when his lips touched her. She felt delirious and couldn't control the motions of her body as she yearned toward him. Suddenly his hands lost the tenderness of their touch and they were hard on her body, pressing, pulling her forward in the chair, and his mouth was at her nipple, his teeth biting, his tongue hard and relentless. She hadn't moved her arms from the chair where he had placed them, but now she threw them about him and pulled his head against her body as hard and demanding as he was, but he slipped away, down, his arms around her, his hands pushing her, his body now between her legs, forcing them wide apart. "No, no, no," she moaned and couldn't move away, couldn't even twist to avoid his mouth and his teeth. She screamed softly when he bit her clitoris. She wanted to cry: not like this, not this way. It's too fast, too excruciatingly intense. She cried inarticulately, and he had one hand loose, massaging the hard bit of flesh that was afire now, and his tongue hot and hard. . . . She screamed again and felt her whole body arch and stiffen, and then she was sobbing and his face was nuzzling her neck, one hand stroking her back and still she throbbed.

She hadn't wanted it like that. She felt cheated and hated him. Her sobs subsided and she started to push him away from her, but his arm tightened and he was lifting her and carrying her to Paul's bed. He put her down and smiled and began to work the bedspread and cover out from under her. She lifted her hips. Now he would cover her and go away and then she would pack up and leave.

She watched him wordlessly. But he threw the spread

and cover to the floor at the foot of the bed. He sat down next to her and he stroked her cheek, down her neck, ran his hand lightly over her breast and let it rest on her hipbone. She began to feel uncomfortable under his gaze and she realized for the first time that the light had been on throughout. She felt herself blush and reminded herself furiously that it was Josie he was making, not her, not Margaret. It didn't really help.

He leaned forward and kissed her right nipple, lightly at first, then harder, and his hand moved, touching her vulva, moving upward. She was too sensitive to stand it. She writhed, and it was starting over again. His fingers this time, his lips hard on her breast, his fingers stiff and hard and demanding, a sudden shift and she knew it was his thumb, his fingers now. . . . "No!" she screamed and couldn't move from him. He laughed and said, "Yes, yes," very softly. "Everything. All the way." She heard her own animal noises and couldn't stop them. She couldn't, not again, she couldn't stand this, she was dying, her heart would rip itself apart, higher and higher, everything was blacking out leaving just the need for release. A scream, the hot flood, even more intense, longer lasting than the first time.

He turned her over and she lay face down, gasping, but there was no respite. He raised her body so that she was on her knees and he was astride her, his hands on her breasts, at her clitoris, in her and out again and again. She passed out briefly and he let her rest, stroking her lightly until she opened her eyes again. "No more," she whispered. "Please, no more."

Even as she said it, his hands were on her again, and she closed her eyes, too weak to move, to resist whatever he did. She knew they weren't through yet, he hadn't come yet, and she couldn't stand any more. She couldn't react any more. Then he was on her, and she felt her body rise to meet his, felt, as if from a distance, the urgency in the motion of her hips, as they moved together.

I had watched the beginning of it but somewhere along the way, I had been drawn in and had been unable to leave her, and now, with this union, I was as helpless as she was. The assault was so total and so thorough that there were no defenses for either of us, and the circles had been narrowed and narrowed until there was just a point that was I. He was hurting her and even the pain was exquisite now, deeper and deeper with a thrust that was brutal. I shared her hurt and her ecstasy, known to her for the first time that night. The climax was explosive. I felt his presence also, here, away from her completely, and while it lasted I was not alone. And that, too, was the first time. I felt his climax and hers and the combined emotional pitch threatened to drown me.

Suddenly it was gone. Everything was gone. I was in the gray area of nothingness. I was alone, lost, bodiless. And afraid.

Chapter 6

The grayness swirled and became solid, a plain that was featureless at first, then with grotesque shapes emerging from it, obviously things growing, but things that shouldn't have been. They looked like monstrous scabs, like leprous fingers curled obscenely in an attitude of prayer, like parts of bodies covered with a fungus or mold, misshapen and horrible. One of them moved toward me and I tried to retreat, but couldn't.

At first there had been nothing, then a visual field with the solidifying of the nightmare shapes on a plain, and now smell was involved. Rank and putrefying, at once moldy and ancient and pungent. And I heard them: the shapes were sighing and moaning, and they were all pulsating, as if boiling from the center, threatening to erupt, subsiding again. Sight, smell, hearing. I tried again to move away. I tried to will them out of existence. Next would come feel and I couldn't . . . couldn't. The first shape that had started to move was closer to me. It hunched itself along like a slug, but it was big. It looked like a disease-ridden organ, a lung, or part of a stomach that was perforated all over. It humped and slid forward, humped and slid forward, closer and closer. It would smother me and I would feel it, die in it.

I had to run, couldn't just stay there and let it cover me over. I had no body, nothing. But I was there and it was coming closer and I knew that whatever it was of me that was there, it would be under the loathsome thing. Fear became terror. There was nothing but terror, would never be anything but terror and the madness of knowing that it was infinite. The thing would advance on me forever and I would wait for it forever.

I was snatched from it, and this time the gray nothing changed again but so quickly that I almost missed it. There was a long wide balcony, sunshine filled, with white marble walls and cool-looking green furniture, a golden floor that dazzled in the sunlight, a white balustrade with white wrought iron in intricate designs. I was alone. It was very lovely. The balcony was quite long and I covered it somehow, as if I were walking on the golden floor, but I was not there, just as I hadn't been in the plain. That seemed the memory of a bad dream now. I was gay and alive and happy. The sun was yellow and threw shadows of the chairs and the beautiful ironwork on the white marble of the wall. Somewhere there was the sound of running water.

The balcony made a turn at the end and I saw fountains, many fountains in tiers, as far as I could see. I stopped and stared at them with delight and very slowly was drawn on. The first fountain was six feet high with three bowls. The water sparkled with multicolored lights, yellow, red. It ran over to the first bowl, filled it and plunged downward to the second, then down again to the third, and each time the lights changed, became dimmer, then more intense. The water flow ebbed and swelled and erupted higher than before. I ebbed and swelled with it. The eruption filled me with pleasure so intense that it was staggering, unbearable. It flowed from me, then started again, to higher peaks; the water shot up higher and higher, straight up in a column, and as I watched it I could feel myself swelling, growing, rising with the column of water. It broke and spilled over, flashing a rainbow of color. An agony of pleasure, unendurable ecstasy. The water started to swell upward again . . . I was drawn to the next fountain.

Silvery water gushed from a narrow opening in a ledge that was covered with moss. The silver water splashed down over worn, green velvet-covered rocks, to a pool, down again in a sheet of water over a straighter smooth face of glistening red granite to another pool, down again to the final pool where lily pads floated serenely. As the water gushed from the opening I could feel myself responding again, even more intensely than before. Pleasure became pain. I couldn't move, couldn't respond. Again and again. There was nothing else, no memories of anything else, no hope ever for anything else. Ebb and flow, surge and erupt, forever and ever. Pleasure into pain, ecstasy into agony. . . .

A shift. I could move. I touched white-hot ground, screamed, jumped, acid everywhere, in the air, in the water. I swam in acid, felt it burn through me, screaming, screaming. . . . Being held softly, probing things getting a better grip, holding tight, pulling in two directions. Screaming. Rods being inserted in me, being twisted and turned and growing, pushing me, splitting me, red hot and hotter still; hanging from rods, spinning around closer and closer to a fire, singeing, roasting, cracking. . . . Running, strips of skin and hair being pulled off, stripping away skin, flesh, muscles; running, trailing bits of flesh, screaming.

On a table, restraints on legs, arms, around chest. Cold something on tongue, in vagina, shock, arching body, screaming . . .

A shift. Cradled in warm arms, loved, safe. Circles widening, an intermixing of two beings, shared joy, shared thoughts, no hidden places or retreats, none wanted. A voice: "You're safe now. See how it can be."

"What has happened? Who was doing all those things to me? Why?"

"Because you were vulnerable. Incomplete. You didn't know the rules and you had to be taught not to wander until you do know them, or any of those things could happen and never stop happening. Or this can happen."

A shift. Gray, alone, nothingness. Afraid. I tried to will something into existence, but the gray remained unbroken. I moved but nothing changed. Where was it? Where was *I*? I moved again farther; the gray remained with me, pressed against me on all sides and there was only the nothingness forever and ever. I called out and heard nothing, not even my own voice. I moved again and called again. I stopped after a long time and I didn't know how long I had been there, I started again, and stopped again. I had no thirst, no hunger, no fatigue. Eventually I stopped moving, stopped calling and did nothing. I pulled a small circle tighter and tighter about me and did nothing forever and ever.

Chapter 7

I didn't feel the next shift. Just suddenly I knew that I was again attached to Margaret, a long way away from her, but I could sense the link; no longer was I lost and wholly alone. I started to return.

Margaret lay on the bed, covered, with her arms lying on top of the blanket, breathing very deeply. I wanted nothing more than to be left alone for the rest of the night to consider what had happened to me, but Morris Stein was still there. He was smoking, seated at the side of the bed, not touching Margaret, but studying her closely. I could feel his presence when he reached over to observe her intently, and when he leaned back. He started to talk, very, very softly, not quite a whisper, but almost.

"So tired. So very tired. Limp all over, exhausted. Too tired to move. You don't want to move a muscle. Too tired to move a muscle ..." That went on for several minutes; nothing else was coming in, nothing from her body at all. I tried to make her legs move, twitch, anything, but it was as if they were disconnected. And the voice went on and on. "Drift, drift, away from everything, don't think now, don't feel anything now. Tired, tired, sleepy. You can hear my voice, nothing else. Nothing but my voice. Too tired to move. Too tired to want to move. ..."

I tried to make her wake up, tried to make her move, to dream. I tried to form a dream, but the relentless voice didn't permit that. "Don't think," he said soothingly. "Just let go and drift now. You don't feel your legs, your arms, you are drifting free of them now, don't think, drift away from your body, away from your hands. ..."

He lifted her hand and it was like a doll's hand. He held it at the wrist and her hand hung limply. I tried to straighten it but his voice was ordering now, "Let go, darling. Just let go all the way. Don't be afraid. Nothing to be afraid of, nothing to worry about, just drift and don't think of anything. Very comfortable, very pleasant now, so nice to drift, not to think." He released the wrist and her hand remained there by itself. I couldn't make it fall, couldn't make it straighten. He took it again and closed her fingers hard, rubbing them several times. "You can't move. Not at all now. You have forgotten how to move for the time being. You can't move a muscle now." He released her hand again and said, "Open it, Josie."

The "Josie" startled me and for a moment I almost pulled away from his voice, but the moment passed and I was trying to open the fingers desperately, and not succeeding.

"You can speak," he said. "When I ask you a question you will find that you can answer with no difficulty at all." He put her hand down on the bed again and opened her fingers. Once more it was like having a doll's hand manipulated.

"You helped Paul with his experiments, didn't you?" he asked then.

I heard the sound of a click, a switch, the tape recorder. I tried again to get away, out of his range, just far away. He said, "Answer me, darling. You did help Paul, didn't you?"

"No, no," I heard Margaret's voice, but the thought was mine. She sounded so dreamy and faint.

"Relax, dear. Relax. It's all right. You are going deeper and deeper asleep now. Deeper and deeper. You will keep hearing my voice, but go deeper and deeper."

I floated, unworried about Margaret, not thinking of anything at all, just free and peaceful. I heard him, but he was talking to someone else, Josie, and I paid no attention. Floating, just floating. He spoke several times calling Josie by name and I ignored him. Then I heard, "When I touch your hand you will wake up. I will touch your hand and count to five and you will wake up. You will feel my hand take yours and you will hear my voice and you will wake up. When I say, 'You are very tired,' you will go to sleep again, but you will hear me and answer me the next time. ..."

I heard everything he said, but he was talking to Josie. It was my hand that felt his touch, however, and when he began to count, I felt myself coming back, slowly at first, then with a rush.

Margaret blinked rapidly and tried to sit up. She saw Morris Stein at her side and shut her eyes tightly. "How do you feel, darling?" he asked her.

Margaret wasn't certain. Strange, she thought, but she didn't say that. "All right," she said. He took her wrist and she knew his fingers were feeling for her pulse. "What are you doing?"

"You are very tired," he said.

There was no resistance this time from either Margaret or me. He talked me into the floating stage and did his tricks with Margaret's hand, and then he said, "You can sit up, get up, and walk around. You will sit up when I tell you to sit up. . . ."

He got her to the chair where she had been when he came in so many hours earlier. He got her into her robe and slippers, and all the while I floated not caring what he did, what he had her do. Then he gave her instructions: she would find that she was remembering everything that she and Paul had done together, everything that he had told her about his work and experiments. She would want to tell Morris about it, nothing about it would alarm her. She would trust Morris completely, feel very secure with him. She would want to talk to him about the experiments, about Paul and his work, etc., etc. Also he told her again that whenever he said she was very tired, she would fall asleep again, that she would always hear his voice and respond, etc., etc.

I heard the back door open and close. Bok was there. He stood inside the door and watched Morris Stein. Morris paused very briefly, then returned to Margaret. He told her that he was going to leave her, that in two or three minutes she would wake up, get up and go straight to bed. That she would not turn off the light. She would forget that he had been there at all that night. She would remember falling asleep in the chair, waking there, and going to bed as usual. That's all she would remember about the night. She would notice nothing unusual about how she felt, about the bedclothes. As soon as she saw Morris the next day, she would ask why he hadn't returned after dinner. I heard him gathering up his things, the tape recorder. I heard him and Bok in the living room, his soft voice saying to Bok:

"It isn't going to be as easy as I thought at first. She's a good subject, but there's powerful resistance to the idea of telling about any of it. She did everything I suggested until that."

Bok's deeper, impatient voice: "Why are you leaving it at that? You had her good and under. Why are you stopping now?"

"There's only so much you can do the first time. I probably went too far with her as it is. Let's wait and see how this takes. She'll be easier and more receptive each time from now on, and I left a cue on her that she can't resist. Give it time, Bok. You've waited this long, a couple of days won't kill you now. Shh."

I had been floating freely, then gradually felt the effects of his voice wearing off, and I was returning to Margaret again. She was starting to feel cramped and cool and she stirred restlessly and opened her eyes. She yawned and pulled herself from the chair. She loosened her robe as she went and let it fall to the floor at the side of the bed. She lay down and pulled the cover over herself and fell asleep almost instantly. During that brief period I had been startled to find myself detached again, although for only a moment or two. I wondered if I would have been able to make her do anything other than what she had done. As she slept I mulled it over.

Bok and Morris Stein were standing together at the open door watching, and when Margaret was obviously asleep again, Morris walked across the room, looked at her closely for a moment, and turned off the lamp. "The real test will come in the morning," he said, and Bok chuckled. They left the house together.

Chapter 8

It was late when Margaret woke up. She stretched and yawned, snuggled down in the covers trying to return to sleep, but gradually gave up and considered the day. Monday. Bok and Morris Stein would be in and out with their work; if it was warm enough she would swim, take a walk, maybe do a little bit of weeding. There were irises along the drive that had become choked with weeds. She got up and showered, humming as the water stung her skin. She felt better than she had for a long time; she had known that being by the sea, alone, away from Bennett and the city would be good for her.

Bennett called just as she was finishing her breakfast.

"Margaret, I'm bringing Greeley out tonight, we'll stay until sometime Wednesday afternoon or evening. God, the man is a dynamo, but it's getting to be too much. We need a place away from reporters where we can talk and just rest for a day."

Margaret sat down on the couch staring straight ahead dully. "What time will you get here?" she asked.

"God knows. I called Lizanne early this morning and

she's on her way, she'll be on the bus that gets into Baiting Hollow at twelve-thirty. I told her to make something that can keep until we arrive, ten, eleven, I don't know. How are you fixed for Scotch, wine, bourbon? Is there any brandy in the house?"

"I don't think so. I'll look. Will it be just the two of you?"

"Most likely. Greeley understands how small the house is, but it seems ideal for this kind of a rest. We might decide to ask a few people in for a conference Tuesday night, but no one else will be staying and Lizanne will take care of any cooking." He paused, and when she didn't fill in the silence he said, "You feeling better now? Resting a lot?"

"Yes, as a matter of fact, I feel very well. This is unexpected. I wish you'd told me sooner. I didn't bring many clothes with me. . . ."

"Don't worry about it, dear. I'll bring you a pretty. Okay?"

She said, "Of course."

"See you tonight, Margaret. I've missed you."

She hung up very gently, hardly making a click. She had to get rid of Bok and Morris Stein, had to change beds, tidy up, straighten up the apartment for Lizanne. She poured a second cup of coffee and took it with her to the living room. It was eleven-ten. Her head started to ache. She found the number of the liquor store in Baiting Hollow, started to dial it, then hung up. In whose name? She couldn't use Josie's name, run up a fifty-dollar liquor bill, or higher even, and if she used her own name, the whole dual role was finished. She sipped her coffee, and her head ached more as she thought of the scene of denouement that was certain to come now. Bok would be furious with her, and Morris Stein ... She lighted a cigarette. The only one of the bunch that she felt she could trust, and she had lied to him too. She had lied to everyone, playing a game with them when they were serious about what they were doing.

I was not surprised at her thoughts about Morris Stein. He had told her she would feel like that; what did surprise me was that I shared those feelings to a certain degree even while I knew I disliked and feared him. She was wondering if she couldn't confide in Morris Stein, explain to him exactly how she had got herself into this situation, that she hadn't meant to hurt anyone, or to embarrass anyone. ... I was thinking that here was a man who was to be avoided. He had used her like so much clay, to be shaped this way and that, to be forced into a mold that wasn't hers at all, then left her there thinking kind thoughts about him. I didn't like his putting her aside and using me as he had done. I made a picture of Gus Dyerman. She refused to see it. He can order liquor for you, I said insistently. She was thinking that she would have to place the order, give her rightful name so they would take her check when the order arrived, and she started to dial.
. . .

I guided her fingers, however, and Gus Dyerman answered the ring of the phone. Margaret stared at it stupidly. "Gus, I'm sorry, I thought I was calling the liquor store. . . ."

"Anything I can order for you, Miss Oliver? Be glad to add it to your regular order. . . ."

Bok and Morris Stein were coming. She had to be on the phone when they got there, it would be a defense against Morris Stein. I made her forget what she wanted to order, and she asked Gus to name various brands until he said the ones that she recognized. Bok's heavy knock shook the door. Margaret looked up, but Gus was speaking and she couldn't leave. Bok and Morris Stein entered the kitchen, came through to the living room. Bok was holding the last notebook that he had taken out with him. She took it and motioned for them to wait a moment. When Gus paused she excused herself from him and covered the mouthpiece with her hand and said to Bok, "You'll have to leave, temporarily, Dr. Bok. My ... nephew is coming this evening with friends. His cook is due to arrive in less than an hour. She'll need the apartment."

"Miss Oliver, you can't be serious!"

She ran her free hand over her eyes. "He called me a few minutes ago. I had forgotten that he said they might come out. I'm sorry. You can return Wednesday night, or better, Thursday." She had kept her eyes on Bok but now looked directly at Morris Stein and she felt something inside her lurch. She frowned slightly; it was gone, and the strange feeling was also gone. She smiled at him and said gently, "You didn't come back for your coffee last night." I couldn't keep her from saying it, but it wasn't the question he had ordered. Morris Stein smiled and lost a little of the watchful look that he had shown when he first came in. He shook his head and inclined it slightly toward Bok, as if accusing him of preventing it. Margaret nodded.

"Why don't you hang up so we can talk about all this," Morris Stein said easily. Margaret nodded and removed her hand from the mouthpiece.

NO, I said. I moved right in on her then and made her remember that Lizanne was due in an hour, that she had to clean the apartment before Lizanne got there, that she still might be able to carry out the masquerade, if she got rid of Bok and Morris Stein now. Right now. She said to Gus, "Can you wait just a minute, some people came, but they're leaving now. I'll just see them to the door." Bok looked murderously at Morris Stein, who shrugged. Margaret put the phone down and went to the back door with them. Bok held her hand a moment and murmured, "Until Thursday, my dear." She withdrew her hand quickly and nodded.

Morris Stein looked at her with a slight smile and also lifted her hand. Margaret was dismayed at the feeling that went through her, and again a faint frown appeared on her forehead. I had been keeping in as close as possible, but suddenly, without any preliminary warning, was detached and I heard myself say, in that distant voice that was hers, yet mine, "Why didn't you come back?" She shook herself and looked puzzled, and forgot what she had asked him.

"Until Wednesday night," he said lightly then. He had been watching her very closely and he was satisfied with what he saw. I listened to them after they left and Margaret bolted the door. Bok was angry and Morris Stein was relaxed, very self-assured. I decided at that moment that I hated the good-looking young man. Margaret returned to the phone with a disconcerting memory of her hand again in his and the feeling of desire that accompanied it. She felt very frightened of Morris Stein, mixed with the feeling of trust and wanting to confide in him. She shook her head in bewilderment and returned to the mundane affairs of ordering wine and liquor.

Lizanne arrived in a taxi and Margaret felt like an

intruder in the kitchen afterward. Lizanne went right to
work checking staples, making a list in her indecipherable
handwriting, stepping around Margaret as if she were a
chair. She told Margaret to leave the beds alone; she
would do them. She collected Margaret's soiled clothes
from the hamper and vanished to her apartment with
them, and she called in the grocery order personally, laps-
ing into French several times when her indignation overcame her. Gus didn't have some of the things she wanted,
and she made substitutions haughtily. She was nearly six
feet tall, as straight as a flagpole, with an incredible mass of
black hair coiled in intricate loops and fastened with large
Spanish combs. Margaret already had stripped the bed in
Paul's room, and collected her things from the room. She
went in to check it once more. Arnold Greeley would have
to sleep in Paul's bed that night. The thought was disturbing.

She took her book and ashtray, and the glass with a
partially finished drink in it and then stopped and stared at
the chair. She had fallen asleep in the chair, had awakened
and gone to bed. She remembered falling asleep in the
chair. The light had been on. She had dozed. Then, what
. . . ? What . . . ? Nothing. She left the room and minutes
later heard Lizanne there opening the window to air it,
and then the sound of the vacuum cleaner. She looked over
Josie's clothing and found a long skirt, raw silk, beige, with
a wide belt. That and her black crepe blouse. And Bennett
was bringing her a "pretty." She heard herself say, "Until
Wednesday night," and she bit her lip. She must be going
completely mad.

Lizanne wanted to make her lunch and she said no, just
coffee. She went for a swim and although the water was

cold, the sun was hot on her when she got out and it was very relaxing. She napped afterward. Lizanne prepared tea and she was ravenous. Then Margaret had nothing to do but wait for Bennett. Lizanne said she would rest until she heard Mr. Bennett come in, and she'd be back. Everything was taken care of. Miz Oliver should rest too, might be up all night with the gentlemen.

Margaret put on records and sat down with a book that she didn't even bother to open. I was going over and over everything that had happened in the last several days, trying to find a defense against Morris Stein. Margaret was trying to find a solution to her problem with Bennett. She didn't like him, but as his wife there were certain advantages, and if marriage would be much the same with any man, the advantages she had with him outweighed the disadvantages. He was generous with her, bought her presents often, liked to take her out to show her off, liked to be seen at openings with her bejeweled and lovely on his arm. They met and talked to interesting people, entertained and were entertained by interesting people. Although he was not an enthusiast, he seemed to understand her love for swimming, and later in the year they would return for a month to the Bahamas, where she planned to take scuba lessons and explore the world under the sea. He thought it an insane thing for her to do, but he didn't really object. Bennett wasn't a bad man, he was kind to children and old people, gave generously to charities, was willing to travel to give speeches for good causes now and then without pay. If she was restless with him, it had to be her fault, not his.

Morris Stein had called me Josie. I was to remember about Paul, his work, his experiments. I ran over the notes

I had seen and could have recited those pages, but that wasn't what he wanted. I groped for something else, all I could remember of Josie; of course I knew nothing about Paul. Margaret was running her hands over Josie's skirt that was heavy against her legs, very expensive, very beautiful. Her blouse was wrong for the skirt, she thought. Something soft, to contrast with the heavy material by texture, not color. She wandered into the bedroom and began to look through the covered clothes again and found a beige chiffon blouse that was meant for the skirt. She slipped it on, tucked the extra inch of the skirt under at the waist and belted it again and then stared at herself in the mirror.

"Josie?" she said, softly, and took a step forward. The mirror blacked out. She swayed. It was daylight, and Paul was behind her, coming toward her, she could see him in the glass. Tall, prominent bones in his face suggesting emaciation, but the arms that wrapped around her were strong and well muscled. She melted into him. I felt him, too. The same thing that I had touched briefly with Morris Stein, a oneness that was abrupt, total, so satisfying that any other kind of existence was barren and unthinkable.

"Meg, darling Meg," he said into my ear, and I pressed hard against his body, my mind and his whirling now, almost dancing, higher and higher. I knew so much, everything he had done, all that he had thought, I knew where we were, and even as I knew it, the gray blossomed and was a garden with birds and butterflies and running water where fawns would drink.

There was no time there, no order, everything was all at once and beautiful. I had been there forever and would be there forever and forever was a twinkling, an eternity.

Paul, naked, bronze, hard muscles and flat planes, ageless; I, also golden tanned, tireless, ageless. Finding answers to unasked questions, not in words, but in a sharing of knowledge and emotions, Eden? For want of a better name, perhaps. How long? As long as you want. Forever! Paul fading, looking from me, a thoughtful expression on his lean face, a question that I couldn't know, couldn't share, expressed in awareness that I didn't have. Paul? Create what you will, Meg, darling. And when you tire of being god . . . Paul fading, looking beyond me, leaving someway that I couldn't understand. Paul? The garden shimmied, then steadied, and I knew that I had recreated it in an instant. I brought Paul back, and tried to dance the circles with him and found only myself there. The garden . . . the garden, I thought sadly and opened my eyes to see myself in the mirror.

I tried to reach Margaret, but couldn't. Whatever had united us was gone again, and she was alone, as I was. Margaret looked deathly pale as she stared into the mirror. She was trembling. Is that what insanity is, she asked the mirror, a retreat from reality into something like that? I wanted to tell her that that too was reality, more real possibly than that frozen image of a woman staring at herself in a mirror. I couldn't get through to her.

She looked ghastly, and sat down at the dressing table to brush color on her cheeks. Her trembling subsided but still she sat there. She had to tell someone. Not Bennett! Their doctor? He'd tell Bennett. Who? She couldn't imagine baring herself to any of the women friends she had, and even less could she talk to any of the male friends. . . . But she had to tell someone. Morris Stein? The flood of relief that swept through her answered the question. If only he were there then, at that moment, she thought bitterly.

I was happy that he wasn't. By Wednesday night another solution might have presented itself. She was too relieved at the thought of confiding in Morris Stein to consider any other alternative now.

Bennett and Arnold Greeley arrived at 10:35. Lizanne materialized to take their coats and pass a tray of drinks and hors d'oeuvres. Bennett kissed Margaret warmly, and Arnold Greeley touched cold lips to her cheek. Supper, Lizanne announced, would be in half an hour, unless Mr. Bennett wanted it later than that.

It was always what Mr. Bennett wanted that counted, Margaret thought, and shrugged it away.

"You're looking lovelier than ever, Margaret," Greeley said, eying her up and down before he sank into the couch. He was a heavy man, six feet, inclined to fat, which he resisted with exercise and a careful diet. He had glasses tucked into his coat pocket, but he could see well enough without them, except, he liked to say, for reading the Bible and fine print in contracts. He looked tired but exultant.

Bennett was studying Margaret also and he said suddenly, "You look wonderful, darling. This rest is agreeing with you." She knew the look, he wanted to go to bed with her right away. She smiled and nodded and said nothing.

"Arnold spoke to a rally in the Garden tonight," Bennett said, drinking long and hard when he paused, "and there was a riot. A real riot."

Arnold Greeley laughed.

"What do you mean?" Margaret asked.

"Oh, the usual. Demonstrators showed up, waving signs

and chanting. They were opposed and the police had to break it up."

She nodded. Bennett looked agitated; the riot had been exciting to him, and he would take it out on her later, she thought. Bennett was only an inch shorter than Arnold, but he was better shaped, with broad shoulders and a flat stomach without diet or much exercise. His shoeshine hair was precisely parted and combed, and his glasses became thicker each year. He couldn't see across the room without them.

"We'll have to remember to catch the news," Arnold said, glancing at his watch.

Bennett got up and turned on the set, and they tried to make small talk over the noise of the closing scene of a western, the commercials, station break, and finally the opening news item reeled off in a staccato, uninflected voice. Lizanne said supper was ready. She scowled when Arnold remained seated. Margaret lifted her shoulders helplessly and Lizanne marched back to the kitchen.

"Why don't you bring the stuff out here?" Arnold said, not turning from the television, but addressing Bennett. "Fix a plate for me, will you?"

Bennett and Margaret went into the dining room where Lizanne had set the table. A bottle of wine was in a bucket of ice. Inside the door Bennett pulled Margaret to him and kissed her again, this time with hurried passion. "You look so beautiful," he said. "God, I hope he wants to go to bed early." He laughed and kneaded her breast.

Margaret moved away and started to fix a plate for Arnold Greeley. "You can go back," she said, "I'll bring in the plates." He smiled at her again and left. Lizanne appeared from the kitchen and I knew that she had been

standing there all along, just waiting for the appropriate
moment to enter. She looked at Margaret sharply and
motioned her back to the living room.

"Go back to your husband, Miz Oliver. I'll bring a
cart." The disapproval in her voice could have meant
many things: that she was furious with them for spoiling
the dinner she had prepared, that she had seen the expression of distaste that Margaret couldn't conceal quickly
enough when Bennett touched her, that she had examined
the sheets that Margaret had removed from Paul's bed?
Probably. She didn't miss much. Other times when Lizanne
had used that same voice on her, Margaret had felt like a
child being reprimanded, but she paid no attention now. I
caught the narrowing of Lizanne's eyes as she watched
Margaret. The bitch was alerted to the fact that something
had happened, I knew, and she would be prying from now
on.

Arnold was sitting on the edge of the couch when
Margaret returned. His face was dark with rage and he
had finished his second drink. A sports announcer came on
and Arnold said, "Those bastards; let them ignore me
now, they'll see. By God, I'll show them. Wait until they
see who's writing platforms, whose hand it is that's arrang-
ing things in the court. . . ." He became silent again when
the news announcer returned, but there were a few local
stories that were of no concern to him and the news was
over. He swore fluently and meanly for five minutes. His
fury included Bennett and others who had been with him
at Madison Square Garden. "I want Floyd out!" he said
after the general castigation that damned equally all his
people. "Goddamned ignorant prick, what does he know
about press releases? By God, I want a PR man that can

deliver. You get me Melville, Ben, or you can get out too. You hear me!"

Bennett looked at Margaret and shrugged. He said, "Sure, Arnold, sure. I'll try ..."

"No, Ben, you won't just try. You get him, or get out!" His voice rose to a near scream. "The best show we've managed yet and they don't even mention it! I told Floyd I wanted pictures of blood being spilled! I warned him. ... Get him on the phone! I'll tell the son of a bitch myself."

"Arnold," Margaret said serenely, "let's have coffee first, then I'll try to reach Floyd for you." She poured coffee and handed him a cup, which he had to take from her, as she was moving away again almost at once. "He's probably got his line busy now trying to find out why the story wasn't aired."

Arnold put his cup down and fished a cigar from his breast pocket. He bit the end off and spat it out on the floor in the direction of the fireplace. "You're right," he said to Margaret. "We'll give him half an hour."

When Margaret handed Bennett his cup, his hand closed for a moment on hers in gratitude. She pulled away as quickly as she could and didn't look at him.

Lizanne moved among them, removing the dishes of barely tasted food. Her face was a mask, but her anger surrounded her like a cloud. She refilled the ice bucket, brought out fresh glasses, and then made faint dishwashing noises in the kitchen, and presently was gone. Margaret was paying little attention to what Arnold and Bennett were discussing now. She had a second cup of coffee, black, when she felt herself becoming very sleepy. She wanted them to go away so she could think about the strange vision she'd had.

"... west of the Alleghenies, you're no use to me," Arnold said and Margaret glanced toward Bennett who nodded. "Floyd is barely comprehensible to them, worse than you." Arnold thrust a paper at Margaret. "Read this aloud for me, will you?"

It was a press release: " 'Today Arnold Greeley accused the federal government of deliberate misrepresentation of the facts attending the Urban Renewal Act and its applications throughout the Midwest. . . .' " Margaret paused and looked up. Arnold was watching her intently and Bennett was considering his fingernails.

"That's enough," Arnold said. He turned to Bennett. "Bring her along," he said.

"Where?" Margaret asked.

"The Midwest tour. Starting week from Friday. Cincinnati, Indianapolis, Chicago, Gary . . ."

"I'm afraid," Margaret said slowly, lying, "I don't understand what you mean."

"I mean that you would be a decided asset to our little group, my dear. We're like a family, Margaret, we've got to help and protect each other whenever we can, however we can. There's me, my wife, Betty, and Betty's good, but you have that Midwest accent that no one ever loses. Frankly, Betty has a face like a harpy, and that quick, high-pitched New England voice that turns westerners off like a switch." He turned to Bennett and asked, "Does she photograph well?"

"Like a model."

"Thought so. See that she gets in the press often, pub shots, you know."

Margaret stared at him in disbelief. "I don't think that I

would be of any use to your ... group, Mr. Greeley. My ignorance in political matters is abysmal. ..."

"Mr. Greeley? What's that? A minute ago you were calling me Arnold." He smiled his publicity smile and leaned forward. "You don't have to know anything about politics, but I suspect that Ben here will brief you on what's necessary for you not to say. See? That's how simple that will be. What I can use from you is that certain warmth that you have. You've got what Jackie had, you see. Presence? Charm? Hell, I don't know what it is, but I know it when I see it. Funny I didn't see it earlier. . . . Anyhowsomeever, you've got it, honey, and you will be the biggest asset to our name. Wait and see."

Margaret shook her head. "I'm sorry, Mr. Greeley ..." She caught a warning gesture from Bennett, but went on, "I'm afraid that I'll have to say no. I appreciate your compliment. ..."

Arnold Greeley scowled and turned a black look toward Bennett.

"I think this is too sudden for her, Arnold. Let me explain to her that it isn't a matter of smoke-filled rooms and loud men drinking and swearing all night, and mean little hotels and all that. Let me talk to her about it. She'll come around, you can count on that."

"I am counting on it," Greeley said. He looked again at Margaret and I could see the appraisal in his eyes and manner then. He looked her over as if she were manacled on the block. Keeping his eyes on her, he asked Bennett, "You two aren't have trouble, are you? If you are, tell me right now. I won't carry you only to have you come up with a scandal that will reflect back on me."

Margaret's face tightened furiously and she stood up. "I

think I'll excuse myself," she said. "I've had a long day." Without glancing back, she left them, and inside Josie's room she stopped and shook hard for a moment. I wanted to pat her on the shoulder, but all I could do was stay in close and wish that she didn't have to feel so alone when she could have used me, or someone. She started to undress, and saw the package on the bed. A long box with a silver ribbon on it. She moved it to the chaise longue without opening it and finished undressing and preparing for bed. When she brushed her teeth and reached for the sleeping pills, I didn't even try to stop her. She did not want to be awake, or wakable, when Bennett came to bed.

Chapter 9

It was a gray, sullen day with fog over the water, obscuring the beach, riding halfway up the bank to the yard. Margaret stood on the upper steps and stared at it, then turned on to the weeds and the irises. She had grime under her nails, and one knuckle was oozing blood that was mixed with dirt. She looked grimly satisfied as she yanked the weeds out and flung them into the driveway to be raked together and burned later. She tried to recapture the brief hallucinatory dream that she'd had the day before, and it was no less real, no less vivid in her memory. It was as real a memory as the memory of the scene with Arnold Greeley. Later, when Bennett had come to bed, the sleeping pills had dulled her too much to let him waken her, so he had simply used her. She felt tears near and worked faster. She had not protested and neither had she complied; she had existed as a thing to be used for a brief period, and then put aside.

I heard Arnold Greeley leave the house and approach her, but Margaret didn't, and when he spoke, she jerked and nearly fell.

"Sorry, my dear. Didn't mean to startle you so."

She stood up and wiped her hands slowly on the jeans that she was wearing, leaving moist streaks of dirt down each leg. Her eyes followed her motions. She fished a cigarette from her jacket pocket and he flicked out a lighter for her. "Lovely morning," she said then.

"Let's sit on the rocks over there. I'd like to talk to you a minute, before Ben gets up."

Margaret started for the rocks with no comment, and he walked by her side, also silent.

"Margaret," he said, after she had sat down, drawing one leg under her, swinging the other one, with her gaze on the thick fog that seemed to be increasing rather than diminishing. "Margaret," he repeated when she continued to ignore him, "I'm going to be quite frank with you. If you persist in refusing to join us, then there is nothing I can do about it, of course. I do want you to understand what I am trying to accomplish, however, before you make any final decision."

"Wait a minute, Mr. Greeley," she said then quickly. "You understand me for a minute. I don't care what you are trying to do, what your final objectives are. I can see what your immediate goals are, and I refuse to become part of it. If you decide to fire Bennett because of me, then that's our problem, not yours." She inhaled deeply, then flicked the cigarette down into the fog.

"I like you, Margaret. Not many people would have the courage to tell me that, especially people in your position. ..."

"What's that supposed to mean?"

"Well, you married Bennett out of nowhere. For love, I presume," he added cynically. "The fact that you're from a family where the highest income in the very best year was under ten thousand had nothing to do with it. The fact that you have minks and diamonds and the kind of security that you never even dreamed of has nothing to do with it. I understand all that. I can appreciate people who climb. I'm a climber myself. Ben's a climber. Everyone who counts is. Oh, we're not all reaching for the same things at the top; you wanted money and security. Ben wants the satisfaction of being on the inside of a power structure, not just a corporation, but the real power structure of the government. I . . . want things too. So we're all willing to use each other to get there, and in this case it happens that we can use each other. Each one of us can get what he wants and needs."

Margaret laughed and for a moment he looked startled, then his mask was back on and he smiled also. "Yes, it's amusing. . . ."

Margaret stood up and noticed that the cloud layer finally was being thinned out by the hidden sun. She would be able to swim later. She said, "You pay Ben well, don't you? How much are you offering me to join also?"

He was surprised again. He hesitated, then said, "What do you want?"

"Oh, I was thinking of . . . roughly, ten thousand a month. Is my charm, warmth, whatever it is, worth ten thousand a month to you, Mr. Greeley?"

He stood up too then, and his face was dark with fury. "You'll regret this, Margaret. You can't toy with me with impunity. We'll let this go for now, but I'll have a talk with Ben. We'll see. We'll see."

She laughed and lighted her own cigarette. "That's why you are such an awful man," she said. "You have no sense of humor at all, have you? I don't know if I believe in God or not, but if He does exist, He has to have a delicious sense of humor. You might bear that in mind, Mr. Greeley. When you usurp Him, you might keep it in mind."

Arnold Greeley started to leave, but he stopped and stood quietly for a moment, then swung around to face her again. "You little bitch," he said. "You sly little bitch. You're whoring around, aren't you? You want me to stir it up between you and Ben. You want him to walk out on you so you can make a killing." He smiled at her and looked up and down her body with an appraising gaze. "I have more important things to attend to right now, my dear. But I'll get back to you. We have unfinished business, you and I. I'll get around to it." He swung away and returned to the house with a jaunty step.

Margaret found that her hands were shaking and she threw away her cigarette and jammed both hands into her pockets. Suddenly she felt cold. Was that what she had been attempting? She couldn't answer.

She remained in the yard for the next half hour, then went inside. She could hear the low rumble of their voices from the dining room as she went to the bedroom and closed the door. When she finished with her shower, Bennett was in the room waiting for her. His face was set in hard lines. "What happened between you and Arnold?" he asked. She was wrapped in a towel, and she pulled it tighter about her and went past him to get clothes from the closet.

"Nothing. He wanted to hire me, but I knew you didn't like the idea of having your wife work, so I turned him down."

"Margaret, for God's sake, be serious." Bennett pulled her around and she looked at him steadily. "He told me that you were insulting, not only to him, but to the whole campaign. Is that right?"

"I might have been. I don't care much for politics, as you know."

"You can't treat him like that, Margaret. He's an important man. I won't have you jeopardizing everything I've worked for."

Margaret wondered why Greeley had gone ahead and told him, then dismissed the thought. She didn't care one way or the other. She said, "He hasn't hired me, Bennett. He hasn't bought me, to my knowledge anyway. You didn't sell me to him, did you?"

"What are you trying to do?"

"I'm trying to understand why I have to take his orders, that's all. I am your dutiful wife, but that doesn't mean that you share me with him, does it?"

Bennett took off his glasses and rubbed them vigorously on his handkerchief. He looked very naked with them off. He looked much younger without them. He said, looking down at the glasses, "He thinks you are having an affair." He jammed the glasses back on and looked at her hard. "Margaret, is there anyone else? Is that why you are different?"

She shook her head gently. "No, Bennett."

He believed her. She believed it herself and her innocence was unmistakable. Bennett stared at her another minute and then caught her to his chest. His voice was thick when he said, "When he said that, it was like a knife in my heart. I felt that I was having an attack. I knew you wouldn't, but still you are different, and that would explain the change, I thought. Margaret, forgive me. I'm tired and he is persuasive, and he made it seem reasonable. . . ."

Margaret nodded. She felt admiration for Greeley for thinking of that tactic so quickly. He understood Bennett thoroughly. If Bennett believed she was seeing anyone else, he wouldn't permit her to remain two hours. He wouldn't leave her, or allow her to leave him. He would simply keep her in sight. He was not jealous, but only because she was his possession, and to admit to jealousy would be to admit that his ownership was not total. This retentiveness, if threatened, would bring him to mount a guard on her if necessary.

She said, "Bennett, try to understand what I feel about this whole thing. I don't have any politics, you know that. I worked, went to school, worked again, and then got married. That's been my life. You don't believe I'm having an affair for a minute. Greeley just can't bear to have someone around who isn't willing to bow, and I won't. Really I won't. Ever since I was a child there's been nothing but war and cold war and more hot war. That's what politicians have accomplished. It goes back as far as history, I know, but I personally can be interested only in what affects me. I look around the city and see the filth and the slums and the rotten lives most of the people have to live, and I think: politics. So your Arnold Greeley wants power, many men do. I know that. Money doesn't mean power any longer. I know that. Politics, successful politics means power. I don't care if Greeley gets his hands on that power. I don't see that he's very different from any of the others. I don't care if you want a share of that power. I was a little surprised, but it wore off. I just don't care. I don't think it matters. But I don't want it. I refuse it completely, absolutely."

Bennett had let go of her halfway through the small speech. He looked angry again. "You can't believe that I want to do something for people? Honestly want to do some good with my life?"

She shook her head. "Call me a cynic, if you like. Or honest. I don't care which."

She let the towel fall then and pulled on her panties. He turned away. She finished dressing quickly. Bennett was staring out the window. He looked at her when she sat down at the dressing table and started to brush her hair. "What has happened to you? You know that something has, don't you?"

She shook her head. "I don't think so. Greeley has talked you into seeing something that isn't there."

"Have you been alone here?"

"I told you a Dr. Bok was coming out to talk about some papers left here by Josie. He did, and brought a student with him. He had a letter giving him permission to study the material, so I let them."

Bennett dismissed Bok. "I met him," he said. "No one else?"

"As a matter of fact, there has been," she said, applying lipstick. "Harry Dyerman, the grocer's son. He's sixteen, seventeen." She touched her eyebrows with pencil lightly and Bennett made an abrupt movement toward the hall door.

"Margaret, I'm sorry. God knows I don't believe you can lie to me. That's one of the things that drew me to you in the first place. You are so childishly honest that you need to be protected. I'm sorry," he repeated brusquely.

Margaret nodded. Then before he left she said, "Bennett, who was Paul Tyson? How did he die?"

"Why?"

"I came across his name in some of the books here. I wondered."

"He drowned. That's what the police said anyway. He was a friend of Josie's. Maybe her lover, I don't know." He seemed to realize for the first time that she had dressed to go out. "Do you have an appointment or something?" he asked. The suspicion had returned.

Margaret smiled and shook her head. "I'm going shopping, just to get out of here so you and Arnold can talk." It was obvious to both of them that she didn't care if he believed her or not. "I'll tell Lizanne not to plan lunch for me," she said as she drew on gloves. "I'll have a sandwich in the shopping center."

Bennett had started to open the door. He let it close again. For a long moment they stared at one another. Again he retreated first. "Okay," he said. "I don't blame you. This house is too small to escape in. See you later."

She shopped for the next hour and bought nothing. Then a fabric shop caught her eye and she wandered in and saw a rack of yarn. She hadn't knitted in years, not since she got out of the cast when she broke her leg at twelve, but suddenly she began poring over the books and she ended up buying a pattern and yarn for a sweater and hat to match.

She returned to the house with her purchase, got on her bathing suit and had a swim. Bennett joined her for a few minutes, not getting in the water, but watching her from the beach, holding her towel for her when she got out. That night two men arrived to consult with Greeley, and for three hours Margaret concentrated on her knitting as their talk swirled about her. At twelve she excused herself and went into the bedroom.

Bennett followed her. Inside the room he grabbed her hard and shook her. "You can't act like this," he said. "You have guests."

"I?" She yanked away from him. "DeSilva my guest? I wouldn't invite that man to join me on a raft in the middle of the ocean, and I would turn down his invitation to join him if he managed to get it first."

"Sh!" He put a slip of paper inside her hand. "Arnold said I should give this to you."

She opened it and read the message: "You have a father who is employed by the city of Terre Haute, and you have four brothers who may wish their sister had been politer."

She handed it to Bennett. He kept his gaze on it much too long, and she waited. Finally he looked up at her and crumpled the note in his hand. He was pale.

"Well?" she said.

He turned away from her and reached for the door. In a flat voice he said, "Arnold wants you to talk to Brannigan in the kitchen while he speaks with DeSilva for twenty minutes or so." He left her then.

Margaret didn't move for several minutes. She stared straight ahead, at the mirror, but blindly; slowly she saw herself appear there from a blank that had gradually faded from before her. During those few minutes I had tried desperately to find the way back to Paul and the garden, or the gray void. This is where she had been standing before, staring ahead in just the same way. This time the image remained hers: Margaret looking very small, almost like a little girl in her mother's dress-up

clothes. The "pretty" that Bennett had brought her had
turned out to be a long black velvet dress, shirtwaist front
cut very low, sweeping skirt, with a wide belt buckled
with gold. Her hair hung loose from a gold clip that
gathered it smoothly off her face.

Margaret concentrated on remembering the peace she
had felt in the garden, and gradually she became very
calm and possessed once more. She looked about the
room, picked up a handkerchief, then left once more. In
the kitchen she moved a chair to the cabinets and put a
can of coffee on a high shelf, then moved the chair back to
the table again. She went to the doorway of the living
room and asked, "Would one of you gentlemen give me a
hand. I can't seem to reach the shelves in this kitchen."
Two of them arose, and Arnold Greeley motioned DeSilva
to sit down again. Brannigan came out to the kitchen.

"Our cook is five inches or more taller than I am,"
Margaret said, smiling. "She puts things away where they
are convenient for her."

Brannigan chuckled and handed down the coffee. "Anything else?"

"I think Lizanne left a tray of sandwiches. I know she
bought some Greek olives. I wonder if they are opened.
. . ."

At twelve-thirty Margaret and Brannigan, laughing, returned to the living room with a cart that held coffee,
sandwiches, small cakes. Greeley smiled at her and motioned for her to sit near him on the couch. Margaret chose
a straight chair near the coffee table and proceeded to act
like a hostess, filling cups, passing the sandwiches. I was
staying very close to her, and she had put herself into a
strange, new mood. I found that she was receptive to me

then. When the talk passed from the local political scene of Atlantic City to the more general scene of the whole state, she remembered what she had read of the effects of pollution on New Jersey's oyster industry, and the erosion of the beaches by the storms of the past year, and the gradual loss of farmlands to industry and roads. For an hour she engaged DeSilva and Brannigan in talk about their own state and Arnold Greeley watched her. Margaret was relaxed, amused and amusing, and interested.

At ten minutes after two DeSilva got up and said that they had to leave. He pressed Margaret's hand warmly. "You coming down to Atlantic City tomorrow?"

"Not this time," Margaret said, making no effort to remove her hand.

"Don't blame you. Might get ugly. But the next time they come through, late summer, early fall, you come along. Show you the sights."

Margaret promised to try. At two-fifteen they were gone and Arnold Greeley started to put his arm about her shoulders. Margaret pulled away. She said distinctly, "Don't you dare touch me. Ever." Greeley laughed and went to the decanter and renewed his drink.

With his back to her he said, "I find it very interesting in what roles various people choose to reveal themselves. Ben convinced me that you are innocent, that you have no secret lover, that you don't give a damn about money, any of that." He lifted his glass toward her then and said mockingly, "I have also found that martyrs are very useful, because their search for martyrdom is never ended until they die. How curious that you refused to martyr yourself for your husband, but not for your brothers and your father."

Bennett said, "Cut it out, Arnold. That's enough. Margaret decided to join us, that's enough."

"I think we should have our eyes wide open, all of us," Greeley said. Margaret turned away and went into the bedroom, leaving him watching her, watching Bennett. After a moment I heard Bennett say, "I'm going too. Do you want anything else tonight?"

Margaret wasn't in bed yet. She had undressed and was wearing a flowered robe and slippers, and was pacing the bedroom.

Bennett stood at the door and said, "I've never seen you like you were tonight. You were wonderful. Thank you."

Margaret stared at him in disbelief. "Is that all?"

"What do you mean?"

"That man is blackmailing me. Or is this extortion? And you say thank you." She laughed suddenly and flung herself down on the chaise longue. "I think I am really going mad."

Bennett pulled a chair close to her and tried to take her hand. She pulled it away. "You have to understand that this is not a game, Margaret. You've treated me like a little boy with a new pastime that would fade away in a few weeks, and it's not like that. . . ."

"I can see that," she murmured.

"All right, you hate it all. Most wives have to put up with things they dislike for the sake of their husbands. You spoke sneeringly about corporation wives, they have to be able to take it, you know. And doctors' wives. From our highest government men right down to the level of small-town mayor the wives have to play their parts."

"I know," she said absently. She was thinking that what had happened to her had nothing to do with her at all, she had been used, had been taken from this place to some-place else by someone else. She had been acting Josie's role. But he, the man in her vision, had called her Meg, darling Meg. It was a hallucination, she reminded herself sharply. Nothing had happened. She had not chosen to have a hallucinogenic experience. It had been done to her. She hadn't chosen to help Greeley. . . . All the choices she had made in her life, how many of them had been real choices? Her school? She had been awarded a scholarship that had been renewed yearly until graduation. Her posi-tion with the computer company had been handed to her by the dean at school. The company had sent her to New York, she hadn't asked for transfer. Her decision to marry Bennett? Was that the only real decision she had ever made in her life?

We were so close then. I had to make her see that "choice" too. I was brutal with her, blanking out Bennett, the room, everything. I made her look at the scene again, made her study the flashing thoughts of guilt that had gone through her mind, to be banished as quickly as they had formed. I pulled out the commitment she had made to herself that night and made her see it for the first time. She had made it, then thrust it away never to be remem-bered again, but to act on her as predictably as Pavlov's bells.

She had forced herself to feel married to him that night, forever, with no reprieve possible. Everything else had been formality only, formalizing what already was a fact. She saw it for the first time.

"Margaret! Margaret! For God's sake what happened to you?" Bennett was shaking her.

Margaret opened her eyes and stared at him. She shook

her head, but this time the memory of that first night didn't retreat into oblivion. She remembered it all very clearly.

"Margaret, you're as pale as a ghost. Are you ill?"

She shook her head. "I'm all right. It is so late. I am tired." She stood up and went to the bed, dropping her robe on the floor as she moved, not thinking of it at all. I could feel Bennett's fear and his indecision. He picked up the robe, watching her. He flung it away from him then and hurried to the bed and sat down by her. She turned on her side away from him.

"Margaret, I'm sorry. I didn't realize what I was doing to you. You don't have to go through with this. I'll make Arnold leave you out of it. I promise you I will."

"It doesn't matter," she said quietly.

"Margaret, this is what he wanted. He wanted to separate us, to bring a rift. He's afraid of you. You're different. He knows you're not afraid of him, and he wants to make you bend a little. You should have gone along with him for now, not made an issue of it. He can't stand to feel rejected. I would have eased you out again. Don't play into his hands like this. We still have each other."

She laughed, again very quietly. "I'm taking birth control pills. I started over a year ago."

"I know."

Even this, she thought without surprise.

"I talked to Dr. Crellen about us, our problem, and he told me he'd recommended them to you. He said they are fertility pills. They are used for both purposes, seems funny, doesn't ..." His voice trailed off, the false note of humor not able to sustain the sentence. She made no response, and after another minute he got up and un-

dressed and got in the bed with her. He had forgotten the
light. I waited with interest, but he only touched her
shoulder and let his fingers slide over her arm. She didn't
move from him, or toward him. He withdrew his hand,
got up and turned the light off, and returned to bed. He
didn't touch her again.

Chapter 10

Margaret dreamed all night. She slept so lightly that everything I did and thought made some sort of impression on her, and she accepted my activities as dreaming. I had tried very hard to find my way back to the garden, but without success. I had seen a lot, and she had glimpsed some of it, and remembered a little of it when she woke up. She garbled it badly, taking a scene from here, a memory from there, a wish, a fear. . . . She wrote down what she could recall:

I was on a boat with Bennett and other men, all smoking cigars, drinking, all watching me for the first sign of loosening up. I knew that they would fall on me and rape me repeatedly if I didn't keep up my guard. I was very excited, aroused and afraid, trying not to reveal myself. Greeley stayed within three feet of me all night. The boat was lost, going around in circles. Then my brother Gary came in and he was wearing two guns in holsters. He stood with one foot on a bar rung and watched them all. Betty Greeley said to Arnold, "I told you she was a

*nonentity, but this is a different woman. I don't know this
woman. Who is she? She's going to drown all of us." I
took one of Gary's guns and shot holes in the boat and as
it sank I started to swim to shore. Paul Tyson helped me
when I grew tired.*

After she finished writing down the dream Margaret
read and reread it trying to puzzle out the various parts.
She folded it and put it in her pocket when there was a
light tap on the door.

"Yes," she said. Lizanne entered.

"Do you want breakfast in here, Miz Oliver? Mr. Bennett said I should ask."

"Coffee," Margaret said absently. She had never asked
for any special service before, had always appeared at the
table when meals were ready, always refused any special
attention. Lizanne nodded, not so much in response to
Margaret as in confirmation of her own secret suspicions.
She left. I listened to her in the hall outside the door. Very
quiet whispers, hers and Arnold Greeley's. They retreated,
but I could still hear them, whispering, agreeing that
Margaret was changed, that she was being secretive about
something. Moving out of range then, no, stopping because Bennett had appeared. Arnold and Bennett talking,
Arnold suggesting that Margaret shouldn't be left alone,
that she didn't look well. Bennett agreeing, relief in his
tone of voice.

When Bennett came in he was carrying the coffee that
Margaret had asked for. She was dressed now, in slacks
and a sweater. He had two cups on the tray. Before he
could say anything, Margaret said, "I had a curious dream
last night. In it you and I were quarreling over Lizanne. I

told you that I would fire her if she didn't catch the bus back to the city, and you said I couldn't fire her, that she was your cook, your housekeeper." She poured coffee.

Bennett said, "I don't want her to leave you here alone, darling. I did tell her to plan to remain until you're ready to go back to the apartment."

Margaret nodded. *"Déjà vu.* Strange, isn't it?"

"Not at all. You passed out, or something last night. Obviously I wouldn't leave you alone. You sensed that and dreamed that dream. Wish fulfillment on your part. You really don't want to be alone right now."

"But I do, Bennett. And I will. In the dream, I said that if she stayed, I'd go to a hotel."

"Margaret, don't be childish. I have already told Lizanne to stay with you. Don't make a scene over it." In the past the matter would have ended right there. How many times, Margaret wondered, had she given in to him not because of anything he said, but because he used that particular tone of voice? She sipped her coffee, watching him over the cup, waiting for him to finish. "Arnold and I plan to leave about two or three," he said. "Come on out and behave now."

"I'l fire her, Bennett," Margaret said calmly. "I really will. And if she won't leave then, I'll call the police and have her arrested as a trespasser."

Bennett blinked and removed his glasses and polished them hard. After a moment he said, "You know you can't fire her. You already admitted that. She's been with me since I was a kid; she took care of me all my life. I know that servants are usually the woman's prerogative, but in this case, I'm afraid your dream was right. She is my cook, my housekeeper. She would laugh if you tried to fire her."

"And if I had her arrested? Would she laugh, Bennett? Would you?"

"For God's sake, Margaret! I don't care if she stays or not! Are you coming out?"

"No. I don't want to see Arnold Greeley. Good-bye, dear. Have a nice trip. Don't get bloodied in the riot." She turned her back on him and opened a book at random, then sat down with it not looking up again. He took a step toward her, stopped, snatched off his glasses again and rubbed them on his handkerchief. I knew he wouldn't fight with her, not with Arnold Greeley outside the door. One simply didn't do that. In a very low voice he said, "As soon as I can get away I'll be back, dear, and we'll discuss this whole situation."

With an effort Margaret managed to remain silent, afraid if she said anything at all, she would say too much, and he might decide to stay with her and discuss the situation. When he finally turned and left, she jumped up from her chair and twirled about the room, stifling laughter. She had beaten him! Bennett had backed down from her! I heard him report to Greeley and Lizanne, listened with interest to the three-sided argument that took place, and regretted it when Lizanne left, to go to her apartment over the garage. She had kept the argument going. When she left, the two men said no more on the subject.

At two-thirty Bennett told Margaret good-bye. He said he would call her daily around dinnertime. He asked her very nicely when she planned to go back to the city, and she shrugged. He didn't want to leave, but Arnold Greeley called him impatiently, so he kissed her forehead and hurried to the car. Margaret watched them maneuver over the driveway, with Lizanne in the back seat, and when the car vanished on the road to Baiting Hollow, she breathed a sigh of relief.

She sang as she stripped the sheets from Paul's bed, and flung open the windows to air the room thoroughly. She vacuumed the rug and dusted, and laid a fire, and then put fresh sheets back on. She had noticed some daffodils on the side of the house, and she went out and cut bunches of them and put them in vases, one for Paul's desk, one for the living room, one for the kitchen table. She ignored Josie's room completely. The telephone rang and she had a lilt in her voice when she answered it.

"Miss Oliver, this is Gus. I . . . Ma'am, I may be talking out of school, but I can't seem to get it out of my mind without I tell you about that cook of your nephew's. She's a real troublemaker, ma'am."

Margaret sat down hard, and clutched the phone harder. "What did she do, Gus?"

"Not so much what she did. She was flittin' around town asking questions, sticking that long nose of hers into your business. You know? Just thought you should know."

"Is she gone now? I thought Bennett, my nephew, was taking her back with him."

"Oh, they dropped her. I steered her to the bus. The local," he added maliciously. Margaret smiled faintly. It would take her six hours to get back to Manhattan on the local.

"Gus, I do appreciate this. I don't know what she was after, or why. As you must have noticed, she is a nosy woman, a strange woman. Thanks, again."

"Yeah. Well, I just wanted to let you know that she's

no friend of yours. She didn't get the time of day, either," he added.

"I'm sure of that."

After Margaret hung up she wondered about the questions Lizanne might have asked. They probably thought she was crazy, or she thought they were.

The room was filling with purple shadows, she thought suddenly. This was how it had looked on those lonely days when Paul had sat here waiting for Josie to come back to him. She watched the shadows deepen and she felt immeasurably sad for Paul, dead now, drowned, for Josie who had run away from it. The telephone rang again, and she swore under her breath at it for disturbing the mood that had been building. She didn't touch it. Probably Bennett, wanting to make sure she was there, was alone there. She went into the bedroom and pulled on a hooded jacket and then left the house, with the phone still ringing insistently.

Fog was coming in again. Here and there patches like clouds formed over the quiet water and whether they grew from within, or were added to from without, it was impossible to tell; they grew larger, not ballooning, but spreading over the water, with a flat top that was like a mesa. When the surface of the water was covered with the white tabletop, it started to rise, very slowly, not noticeably except in the way that it climbed up the shore toward the rock where she was sitting. When it touched the rock, she moved to the steps that led up to the yard, and the dense white fog followed her silently, slowly. Margaret let it touch her toes, then moved again, and the fog drove her up the steps, one by one, until she stood in the yard. She waited for it there, and finally walked back to the house in the center of a small circle that was walled by white.

There were no sounds anywhere; the last noise she had heard had been that of a foghorn, very distant, very melodious in its lonesome urgency. The cry of a lost boat. She had recaptured the mood that had started earlier, and when she reached the house, she lifted the phone from the receiver, and then bolted the doors and drew all the drapes.

It was seven and she was very hungry. Secured from the world, she prepared a scant dinner and ate it, and then lit the fire in Paul's room and got out the letters that she had not finished reading. She held them unopened in her lap for several minutes and leaned back and closed her eyes.

I was content also. I searched for the boat that was lost in the fog and found it again. On the rocks, left of the steps that would lead the survivors up here. I found another fog much like tonight's that had covered Terre Haute in late winter when Margaret was growing up there. Lost in the fog, found by a brother and her father. Margaret remembered the incident with just a trace of surprise. She hadn't been thinking of her father or brothers, or home. She didn't linger over it, but released it again almost immediately. She was deliberately giving herself up, willing a passivity of mind. I went outside to look at the small house, pressed in, isolated by the fog, hidden from the world by the fog, and she accepted this image, and didn't turn loose of it. After a few more minutes, she opened her eyes and lifted the last letter that she had read, just to be certain that she had them separated. Then she started on a new one. Josie's letter to Paul. Dated Nov. 29.

Sleet and rain all day, damn, damn. I can't get warm. I can feel my arms and my toes and I know that they aren't really cold, but I am chilled through and through. And when I go to bed, I shiver and can't stop myself from reaching for you, can't stop my feet from exploring, searching for a warm body to snuggle against. You always are so warm. I wasn't going to write to you tonight, after all, I just talked to you an hour ago, but here I am anyway. I love you, Paul. I hate it, I wish I never had met you, but instead, I love you. I can see your scars, and I want to kill anyone who would hurt you. I can feel your warm body, and I could die thinking that others had felt it. I saw Sid Reisman today and he said to tell you hello. But with that look, condemning me, hating me, blaming me, certain that I keep you from your real work. I am jealous of your past, your friends, your colleagues, even your memories. If I could reduce you to a tiny fraction of yourself and keep you in my pocket, I would do it. And never let you go again. See, this is why I have to write to you tonight, my darling. You should know this side of me, too. Possessive, jealous, irrational, totally selfish. I would even take away your books, your work if I could. Anything that might ever come between us in any way. Why didn't you tell me not to come back to the city this week? Why didn't you show just a touch of this kind of jealousy? I am wild with the idea that you wanted to be rid of me, that you are tired of me already.

The letter ended there. No signature, nothing else. Margaret folded it slowly letting her fingers linger over the folds, running her forefinger over the crease. Poor Josie, she was thinking. That had to be the beginning. Later Josie had accepted his work, their separations. But to be so hurt in the beginning, so hurt by love.

Sid Reisman, I was thinking. Sidney Reisman ... then I found it, a column in the *Times*, crediting him with a new discovery in astronomy, radio astronomy. He was a physicist, and had worked out a theory to account for the frequency of certain signals that were being received from a dark source in the constellation Cygnus. There had been a continuation of the story, page 49, but Margaret hadn't turned to 49, and I didn't know the rest of it. Where else? In one of the notebooks at least, possibly more than one, if "S" meant Sid. Paul had made notes about Sid and about someone he abbreviated "S." Margaret had flipped through the pages too fast; I hadn't been able to read anything on them, just a word or phrase here and there. I was determined that she would go back to the notebooks, but I knew it would not be that night. There was too much else coming up that night for her to bother about them.

She picked up another letter, another one of Josie's, and started to read it.

Darling, the crocuses are blooming, aren't they! Last night working late with Tod, suddenly I lost sight of everything around me and all I could see was you, kneeling by the crocuses, holding one in your hand. I know! I know! Two more days and I'll be home. Thank you, darling. Thank you.

Margaret stared at this one, and reread it slowly, puzzled and disturbed by it. I was listening to another noise now, not the crackling of the fire, or the soft rustle of note paper and envelopes, or the squeak of the chair when she moved, but the sound of water slapping the gunwale of a boat, and voices that were at once excited and subdued.

I heard the first grinding sound of the boat on rocks, knew when it pulled loose again, heard the motors in reverse, and again the unmistakable sound of keel against rock. This time the motor didn't succeed in freeing it, and Margaret looked up with an intent look on her face. I knew that she had no idea of what it was yet, but I turned her on full alarm anyway, and she jumped up and ran to the door, still not really hearing anything. When she opened the door, the sounds were audible, if faint. I don't know how I would have got her out if they had remained subliminal, but it didn't become an issue. She ran back to the bedroom and grabbed up her jacket, sped to the kitchen and found a flashlight, and then was running through the heavy fog toward the beach steps.

The flashlight hit the fog and was stopped as if by a wall, so she kept it to the ground where the circle now was very small, not extending more than a half foot from her in any direction. The light did pick up the white of the flagstones that made the path. When she felt that she had to be near the steps, she slowed to a crawling pace and groped with each foot before she took a step. She didn't want to plunge down the rocks to the beach below. Finally she felt the edge of the yard and drew back her foot quickly. She didn't know if she was to the right or the left of the steps and she couldn't remember a thing about how the grass ended, where the last flagstone was, how the first step felt.

There was a faint scream, a woman's scream, from the beached boat, and somehow Margaret found that she was going down the steps. As soon as she took over again it became a hazardous trip, but there was another shout from the boat, and I took her down the rest of the steps quickly and turned her left at the bottom.

She called then to the boat and stopped to listen. They heard. "Hello," she yelled again. She didn't know what she could do for them, other than call out.

"Where are you?" A man's voice.

"Oh shore. Are you on the rocks?"

"We hit a rock out here. How far is shore?"

Margaret was walking carefully now toward the line of rocks that extended out into the water for fifty or sixty yards. Their voices sounded so faint, she couldn't be certain that they had hit these rocks. They might be far out in the water, their voices carried by a freakish fog. I made her look at the picture of the water as far as she could see it; there were no rocks that showed anywhere, except this one pile. She yelled, "Is the rock you hit above water?"

There was silence for what seemed like a very long time, then the answer came, "Yes, part of it, a little bit."

She stumbled then over the first of the rocks and caught herself before she fell down. Her flashlight hit the rock and rang on it. The light didn't go out. She called to them, "The rocks stay above water all the way in to shore, about fifty yards or so. Can you get on them and follow them in? Be careful, they're awfully slippery."

A new voice yelled, "Wowie! Fifty yards. We can swim in."

Sound of several other voices too faint to catch words, then the familiar one. "We're coming in on the rocks. There are five of us. Can you yell now and then so we can keep a bearing on you?"

"Good luck," she called back. "Actually it isn't very

deep here, but you could get turned around and go the wrong way, I guess."

There was a soft scream and a laugh that held a touch of hysteria.

"Keep on your left of the rocks," Margaret yelled, just to be yelling something at them. "They spread out when you get in closer and there are some breaks where you could slip down between them." She was sure that much of what she said was lost in the fog, but she kept on calling, yelling to them.

There was a grunt, and a splash, followed by a flurry of curses and questions: "Clive? Are you okay?" "Yeah, shit, it's cold. Look, take this case, will you." "Yeah, I can get back. Keerist! That's cold!" Margaret was climbing the rocks then. She got to the top and tried to force her light to penetrate the fog, to help them, to see them. Nothing.

"Are you all all right?" she called. She began to inch forward, slowly, very carefully.

"Yeah. Clive slipped, but we caught him." Then: "You sound different."

"I'm on the rocks too now. You must be nearly in." A girl gasped and there was the sound of feet scrabbling on rocks. A stone clattered and made a splash. "Be careful," Margaret cried. "You're very close now. Don't rush." She moved her light back and forth very slowly, and one of the girls suddenly said:

"I see your light. Are we out of the water yet?"

"Not quite." Margaret could hear the man's voice now, speaking softly, almost steadily to the group. He must be leading, she thought. The voice grew stronger and she remained quiet now. They were coming in by her light. She stopped moving toward them and waited. Then she saw a faint blur moving and she knew that they were with her finally.

"I didn't come out very far," she said. "You're almost to the beach now." The blur came in closer and she felt a hand on her hand holding the light. He squeezed her hand, followed it up her arm and then was visible as he moved another step.

"Hi," he said, and his hand touched her cheek briefly and then he turned to help the girl coming up behind him.

"Boy, are we ever lucky you were here!" the girl said. She came into view as a spectral form with flowing white hair.

"I'd better move on, out of the way," Margaret said. "Take my hand," she said to the girl. "It's dry from now on, but still slippery in some places, and you can't see a thing."

The girl's hand was icy in hers, and she wondered at the touch of the man's hand on her cheek. His fingers had been warm on her cold face. She shone the light down on the rock and picked her way back. She didn't recognize the smooth boulder she had been sitting on the day that Morris Stein had found her, but I did, and I turned her there. It was easier going down there than the way she had come up. She slid down first, then came one of the men, the girls and the other two men. They all laughed and joked now, and they all wanted to touch Margaret, kiss her, hug her, shake her hand.

The man who had done the yelling said, "Do you have a car around here, a house, something? What are you doing here?"

"House," she said. "But it isn't going to be easy to find

the steps. They're to the right about two hundred feet from here, I think."

"Let me," he said and took her light, and her hand. "Everyone take a hand," he said. "We've come this far, let's not lose anyone now." There was giggling and again the touch of hysteria from one of the girls, and they started to move up the beach. The icy hand of the girl chilled Margaret. "How long have you been out here?"

"We were lost for hours," the girl said. "Just going around and around in the fog. Something on the boat broke and we were afraid to just stop, afraid we'd be hit. Clive said he knew this stretch of beach," she added, but without rancor.

They found the steps and got up them without mishap, and it was only minutes then until they were inside the house and Margaret had guided them to the bathroom and robes and towels, clothes for the two girls. One of the boys built a fire in the living room and they all took turns roasting themselves before it. They were a bunch of kids, Margaret realized, except for the one man who had talked to her through the fog, and he wasn't much older, perhaps her age, middle twenties or so. The girl with the white hair was no more than seventeen, she was certain, and the other one, black-haired, was possibly eighteen, and the boys under twenty. Clive was tall and built like a football player, and the case he had worried about was a guitar case. Even before he had thawed out, he took the guitar out and began to pluck at it anxiously. It hadn't got wet. He had long hair that he tossed out of his face from time to time, but mostly seemed to ignore. The other boy was shorter and more slender and he had lost a contact lens somewhere out in the fog. He apologized to Margaret when he bumped into her for the third time as he brought in logs for the fire and she couldn't keep from comparing him to her youngest brother, Timmy. Timmy was like a teddy bear too, not quite sure of what to do with his feet and his hands, forever putting them in the wrong place at the wrong time. The boy's name was Mike. The two girls were Ronie and Dale. The man was John Llewellyn.

John Llewellyn smiled at her after the introductions had been made, and said, "Your turn."

Margaret opened her mouth, then shut it again. Who was she to these young people? In fact, she said to herself, rephrasing the question, who was she to herself now? Ronie, the girl with the long white hair and the childlike face said, "It really doesn't matter. You can be anyone you want to be. This is a magic cottage in fairyland, quite invisible, you know, until you get inside it."

Clive strummed several chords, then sang: "We were plucked from the bosom of Neptune. We were plucked from the bosom, plucked from the bosom, plucked by the queen of the fairies."

They all laughed and Margaret said, "Meg Fowler." It was her maiden name, and Meg was what Paul had called her in another fairyland. Suddenly she felt that she really was Meg Fowler. "Now, do you want coffee, hot chocolate, sandwiches, soup . . . what?"

"Coffee," the answer came almost in unison. "Can I help?" That was Dale, the girl with the black hair.

Margaret shook her head. "You'd better dry your hair," she said. "It won't take long." John Llewellyn followed her into the kitchen. At the doorway he paused and asked, "You do have a telephone, don't you? The kids should call home probably."

"On the end table, with the receiver off, but it's in order."

He nodded, as if everyone kept the receiver off the phone. He spoke to the kids again, then rejoined Margaret in the kitchen. "I'll have to call the Coast Guard, I guess, after they get through. I'm going to need help to get the boat off the rocks."

"Maybe high tide will float it off," Margaret said.

"Possibly, but I don't think there's enough variation here to count on it. Clive," he said then, shaking his head. "He used to live up here. He was so sure that we'd just run up on a beach and walk away from it until tomorrow."

Margaret was becoming increasingly nervous, not the sort of nervousness that makes her drop things, or bite nails, but rather showing itself as a twitchy feeling in her stomach, and an occasional quickening of her breath. Some people would have called it a premonitory sensation, but Margaret didn't believe in premonitions.

As she busied herself making coffee, slicing ham and getting out cheese and bread, I studied John Llewellyn carefully.

He was very tall, over six feet, and he needed to gain ten to twenty pounds, but was very well put together anyway. He was wind-burned, with high cheeks flushed dark red, and his hair showed the effects of mist and salt spray, obviously looking darker than it would when washed. It was heavy, rather long hair, straight, and now every which way. He ran his hand through it carelessly now and then, absently, not thinking of it, but bothered when it came down into his face, or tickled his ear. He had the steadiest gray eyes that Margaret had ever seen. When he looked at her, she felt there was nothing he couldn't see in her with those steady eyes.

They talked, but when they weren't talking, Margaret couldn't remember what it was that they had been saying. She finished the tray and he took it from her and carried it to the living room where they were greeted with cries of delight.

The room was changed by their presence. The fire was big and loud, the kids were happy and hungry and at home with Margaret; they all talked with their mouths filled, all at once, no one apparently listening to anyone else. Clive sang when he finished eating, and Margaret refilled cups, and then sat down on the floor with her back against the couch and listened to Clive. There were a lot of jokes between songs, allusions to happenings that Margaret knew nothing about, and very gradually she came to know that they were students, that John Llewellyn was either a teacher, or a counselor, but whatever it was, he was responsible for them, that none of them had classes on the next day, but had to be back at school in the afternoon for play rehearsals, or something.

John Llewellyn heard the car turn into the drive almost as soon as I heard it, and he looked at Margaret, but said nothing when it was apparent to him that she was unaware of it yet. I heard Morris Stein and Bok get out, approach the house, and stop when they heard the music and laughter coming from the cottage. When Morris Stein knocked at the door, Clive stopped in mid-chord and Margaret jumped.

I watched the expressions that the kids hadn't learned yet how to hide, and Margaret caught some of it also. She had become pale at the sound of the knock, but now she flushed and quickly she excused herself and left the room. John Llewellyn followed her. It was almost twelve.

Margaret admitted Morris Stein and Bok, turned to introduce them to Llewellyn, and realized that they all knew each other. Bok was scowling at Llewellyn, and Morris Stein had shaken hands with him very briefly, and then sat down on the edge of the table, waiting for Bok to take it.

"This is a surprise, Dr. Llewellyn," Bok said slowly. "I had no idea that you were interested in Tyson's work. ..."

Margaret felt as if she had stumbled into the middle of a dream, someone else's dream. She looked to John quickly, but he shook his head. "Tyson?" he said, frowning. "Paul Tyson?"

Bok turned from him impatiently and said to Margaret, "I understood that I had exclusive access to the material at this time?"

"I didn't say that," Margaret said. "Anyway, John ... Dr. Llewellyn is here by accident, with several students. They were shipwrecked on my beach."

Neither Bok nor Morris Stein believed her, and Bok regarded her for another moment, then shrugged. "In that event, would you mind if we take some of the notebooks with us now? We have lost a lot of time. ..."

I had been searching, around and around, and I knew that it wouldn't matter if she gave them the notebooks, so I didn't stall her with them, but Margaret hesitated. She was afraid that when she left, in the conversation that was certain to take place between the three men, the confusion over her name would come out, and then the rest would follow. I was watching Morris Stein, and he was clearly puzzled by her, by something that he couldn't understand about her—the difference that Bennett had talked about, that Greeley had sensed in her? Probably. But it bothered Morris Stein even more than it had either of them, and he was feeling responsible for it. He wanted to go with her, I could tell, and I knew I couldn't allow that. Five minutes with her and the game would be up. He was too curious not to put her under and ask pointed questions. I could almost follow his thoughts, and before he could open his mouth and say anything, I turned Margaret and practically shoved her from the room. I knew that the three men were startled, and I tried to hear their talk, but the kids in the living room had started to sing again, and their words were lost to me.

When Margaret returned to the kitchen with three of the notebooks John was saying that he and the boys would wait until morning and the lifting of the fog to see if they could float the boat again without help, but in any event they would all have to leave early in order to be back at the school by afternoon. Bok took the notebooks, nodded a goodnight and left. Morris Stein hesitated only a moment, then also left when no one invited him to stay. Margaret bolted the door after them.

"I was going to offer the bed in the apartment to the boys," Margaret said, "but that's impossible now. Dr. Bok and Mr. Stein are staying up there."

"If you have extra blankets, and don't mind their sleeping on the floor by the fire, they'll be okay," he said.

Margaret nodded and turned to go back to the living room, but he caught her arm and said, "They can wait for a few minutes. Do you mind if we talk a minute first?"

They sat down by the table and he looked at her directly again, and she knew that she would tell him whatever he wanted to know. "I know about Paul Tyson," he said after a moment. "He was a great man, and maybe he was right. I don't know about that. They called you Josie, but you're not Josephine Oliver, are you?" Quickly he shut his eyes and said, "No, don't answer that. It's none of my business. Sorry." He looked at her again and smiled, and the pounding of her heart became normal once more, as quickly as it had exploded into a wild flurry. "I don't care who you are. To me you're Meg. That's enough. Be careful of those two men, Meg. That's all."

She nodded. "They called you a doctor, too. Of what? Are you a physicist?" She was thinking of the letter, and the name of Sid Reisman, even though she hadn't made that connection consciously.

John smiled again. "No, nothing like that. I'm a chaplain. Doctor of theology."

Chapter 11

Margaret was sleeping in Paul's bed, the girls in Josie's bed, and on the living room floor the boys were rolled up in blankets, while John was stretched out on the couch. He wasn't asleep, but was staring at the ceiling, thinking, wakeful dreaming, or in meditation. I couldn't tell which, but by the sound of his breathing, I knew he was not asleep. I could sense his presence in the house, all around the house, and it was as if I brushed something now and then that hadn't been there before, as if a part of him circled also and we had collision orbits, or near collision, close enough to feel each other's passage. I tried to reach him and couldn't; there was only the feel of his presence nearby.

The apartment over the garage was quiet after having had lights on and talk continuing for hours. A wind was starting to blow, and the fog would be cleared before morning; waves were slapping against the boat, the rocks, lapping the beach; the pine trees were awakening to the wind, rubbing needles making sighing noises, an occasional snap of a twig, momentarily restrained, becoming free.

It had been a long day and there was a lot to put in order, to sort and sift and think about. And all the while I was floating in widening circles, looking, not searching then for the grayness, not yet, but suddenly being in it.

Lost, drifting, familiar, and always new, strange and frightening. No contacts now with anything, no self, no body, nothing. Drifting aimlessly because there was no place to go, nothing to see, nothing to do, no past, no future, not even a present. Then, as if it were something I always had known, but had forgotten momentarily, I knew that if there were to be anything, I had to make it. I created a meadow, green grass sparkling with dew in morning light, warmth of fresh winds blowing softly. I made a beautiful city off in the distance, with spires alight in the rising sun. I added a brook, to give sound and movement to the scene, then some trees, and a whole forest stretching to one side, with fearless animals there, and birds of every hue, and butterflies. I was still nothing but an awareness, so I brought Margaret's body to the garden and ran my hands down over the smooth warm body that was also me. But as I made the garden in front of me and created myself again, I felt that everything was slipping away from behind me and I spun around in time to see the gray that had been advancing stealthily. I banished it. Now for Paul. I brought him back, golden bronze, alive.

"Paul!" I flew across the grass to him. "I missed you so! Don't go away. Ever."

"I missed you," he said. "Don't you go away."

I threw myself at him and his arms caught me and held me close and when I lifted my face, he kissed me. I burned and ached and his kiss chilled me. I stepped back aghast and stared at him, through him. "You're not real, not really here at all." He vanished. I whirled to see the gray take away the garden, the trees, creep over the brook, erasing it as it touched it. "Back, get out!" I screamed at it and it was gone again. I made the meadow come back and the forest, forgot the brook, and had running water that ended abruptly, not going anywhere at all, just stopping. I stared at it, and made a hole in the ground and watched it plummet downward. I let earth slide down the hole, the carpet of grass flowed toward it, was channeled and slid out of sight, then came the trees, holding their branches in close to their sides as they started downward; the birds were caught in a whirlpool and fluttered in narrowing circles, unable to escape, down. When finally there was nothing left, I felt myself being drawn to it, and helplessly I yielded. I dissolved and flowed toward the hole, gathering momentum, through it, down, spun as if in a centrifuge, faster and faster.

It was my world, I had created it, and now I was lost and falling through it, just as my trees were, my animals, my grass, my city. "Out," I screamed at the city that was swirling about me. "You don't exist!" It was gone. I banished everything. I was falling alone, no longer buffeted by my own artifacts. I couldn't stop. "Paul! Somebody! Help me! Please help me!"

I don't know how long I cried for help, but after I had fallen through the entire universe, someone was with me, someone who was breaking the fall, slowing me down, supporting me. "Easy, easy," he said. "It's all right. I'm here."

"Who are you?" I couldn't see him, or anything else,

but he was there with me. "Where are we? How did you get here?"

It was John, I realized. John Llewellyn. "But I thought only dead people were here!"

"You brought me to you," he said. Where earlier we had been in collision orbits, now the orbits were united, each of us contained within the other. There was only one being now, not the two separate ones that had gone to that place alone and apart, but something else that was more than the simple conjoining of its two parts. We created a world that was whole and beautiful and very real, and we peopled it and we lived in it forever and ever, and it was very good. And one day he looked past me, and I felt myself being wrenched in half, divided once more into an empty, unfinished, aching being that yearned to be whole again. I saw him standing apart, looking beyond to a point I couldn't see, couldn't understand, and he began to fade, and when he faded, the world dissolved and became mist that rose in tendrils that were lost in the gray. I wept.

Margaret stirred restlessly, but didn't wake up. Then she sat straight up, the kids were singing again. It was dark still, not morning yet, but they were singing and laughing in the living room. She floated from the bed to the door to peek out through the crack. No lights were on; the fire had been rebuilt and lighted the room with shifting red lights. Ronie was dancing, naked, her white hair down both shoulders covering her breasts, her narrow hips moving spasmodically in rhythm to Clive's guitar. Margaret stared. She moistened her lips and couldn't take her eyes from the undulating body of the girl writhing before the fire. She joined the group in the living room, the distance that had separated her from them melting away without any motion on her part. Everyone was naked, she realized, and made a tentative movement toward the gown that she wore. John pulled the straps from her shoulders and the gown fell down her body softly, settling about her feet. She stepped out of it. Ronie continued to dance, her eyes open, watching Margaret. I felt the searching intensity of her eyes and I moved Margaret toward her. Ronie was tiny, beautifully formed, with suntanned legs, white belly and breasts, suntanned shoulders, strap marks. Margaret touched her lightly on the shoulder, and it was as if she had been touched. She felt the girl's warm skin under her hand, and felt her own skin responding to the touch of another. Suddenly she was feeling the girl all over unrestrainedly, and the girl was quickening to her fingers, her heart pounding visibly, making a pulse between her breasts, her breath coming in gasps, a flush on her cheeks now.

Ronie's pubic hair was as white as the hair on her head, and soft like rabbit fur. Margaret's fingers smoothed it, then wound it in little curls, then smoothed it again. Ronie's hands were on her now and the heady, intoxicating flood of desire rose in regular waves, each higher than the last, wrenching her from her groin, from her vagina, upward, making her suck in air, causing her heart to pound hard, then almost stop, only to pound harder. Ronie's slim fingers traced her nipples, and then her white teeth caressed them more delicately than her fingers had. Margaret tasted the girl's skin and her hand began to massage her vulva gently. Her fingers found the tiny clitoris, hard, rigid, almost miniscule, and Ronie jumped and exhaled a long sigh of pleasure.

"My God, she's beautiful," someone said, and Margaret

knew they all were watching now. She didn't leave the girl. They were lying on the blanket before the fire, and the play of firelight on the girl's pale body was more exciting than her touch had been. Ronie's body was working, moving upward and back, from side to side; her eyes were partially closed, her mouth slightly open. Margaret kissed her lips, forced them apart and found Ronie's tongue hard and responsive. Her fingers were inside the girl now, and it was hot and wet and, and suddenly contracting in convulsive waves, and Ronie screamed.

Margaret didn't remember getting to her feet. Someone led her back to her room. She was knotted inside, weeping, sobbing. Behind her the kids were laughing; one of the boys was with Ronie now, the other pair coupled on the couch. There was a lot of laughter from them all. John pushed the door closed to Margaret's room, then lifted her and kissed her long and hard. The knot exploded, shattered, hurling Margaret from his arms. She was stretched out in the bed, her legs wide apart. When he touched her, she wanted to feel him, to know his body with her hands and her mouth, just as he was knowing her body. She wanted to have his penis in her hands, to kiss it, to caress him with her tongue. The thought overwhelmed her, but she didn't move, and her body was trembling now under his hands and his mouth, and still her thoughts continued: what would he think of her if she touched him, what would he do? It was too late now. Her hips moved, her body surged toward him; the crescendo was on her, and the world was gone, everyone was gone, everything, leaving only the rising, thundering end. Suddenly he withdrew. She clutched at his hips and tried to pull him back to her, but he gently placed her legs together, kissed her lightly on the lips, and left the room, making no sound at all when the door closed.

"No!" she screamed, and sank into unconsciousness.

I heard John stir, come to her door and listen outside it for a minute. He whispered her name, then opened the door and looked inside. He approached the bed, stopped halfway into the room and looked at her for another minute. She was unmoving, only her hands betraying her newly relaxed position as each of them uncurled from a tight fist into the tonelessness of one deeply asleep. He left as quietly as he had entered.

Margaret stirred, and waves of desire returned as wakefulness tightened her muscles once more. I knew she couldn't handle the memories, so I put them out of reach and she was left trembling with sexual desire with nothing to relate it to. She sat up and hugged her arms about her shoulders and rocked back and forth for several minutes, but she knew she would not go back to sleep. It was almost dawn.

After a few minutes she was too restless to stay in the bed any longer. She got up and dressed, then opened her door very quietly so that she wouldn't waken the boys sleeping on the living room floor. She paused a moment before the kitchen door. It was closed. John Llewellyn had said that they would all be up early to try to float the boat again. I knew that he was already in the kitchen, sitting at the table drinking coffee, reading one of Paul's notebooks. When Margaret opened the door she was not surprised to see him either.

"Good morning," she said in a whisper, pulling the door closed again quietly. "You're up awfully early. Did you sleep all right on the couch?"

He hesitated, studying her, but not obviously. "I had dreams," he said finally. "You?"

She moved from the door and, still whispering, said, "I've been dreaming a lot since I came here. It must be the sea and the wind."

"Maybe." He didn't believe it. "I made coffee. Do you mind?" He motioned toward the living room. "You don't have to worry about them. I'll have to pound on them to get them up later."

Margaret grinned and took the cup of coffee that he had poured for her. She indicated the notebook. "Do you understand what he was doing?"

"I think so, some of it anyway. I heard him lecture when I was a student, eight or nine years ago."

"Will you tell me about it?"

"That's the hard part. It's like saying, tell me about God, and that stops me cold too. Let me think a minute." He leaned back and stared ahead for a minute, then said, "Tyson had a theory that there is actually a higher consciousness much as the mystics talk about it, and metaphysicians and so on, but he didn't think it was a state of mind that required years of study to achieve. And he thought that drugs were the wrong way too. In fact, he tied it all with the way that we perceive time, or the action of time, and he felt that if we could look at time from a different angle, or with a different psychological set, then we would be able to see that there is this other dimension that exists all about us, but that we blinded ourselves to it deliberately in some distant past as a matter of expediency." He smiled apologetically and shrugged, "And that's about all I know of his work. He didn't publish

much, and of course he died suddenly leaving it all very
much in the air."

Margaret had grown tense with his words and now she
relaxed again. "A mystic?" she murmured. "I thought he
was more ... oh, different. I don't know what I thought
about him, but not that. That sounds like the kind of stuff
that's always being written about in paperback books with
big eyeballs on the covers."

John laughed. "Paul Tyson was one of the great physi-
cists," he said. "He worked on the bomb, for heaven's
sake, and then retired with a mild heart attack and devoted
himself to the study of time. He lectured a little, when he
felt like it."

She felt chagrined and said ruefully, "And that points
up my ignorance." She picked up the notebook and let the
pages riffle. "I tried to read through one of them, but the
figures he used, the math and symbols ... I got absolutely
nowhere."

"I think his contention was that if one person could
understand the process, he could demonstrate it and teach
it empirically, so that further understanding, while always
desirable, would not be completely necessary. The hard
part, the part he had to do, was to change his own method
of perceiving. It's like a religious conversion, I guess. Has
to go all the way through every layer, or it doesn't take. So
he amassed all this data," he pointed to the notebooks,
"and he lived with it until his world view must have been
unlike that of anyone else on Earth. He deliberately chal-
lenged the concept of the present as the past becoming the
future. And that's the basis of Western civilization." He
closed the notebook that he had picked up, and shook his
head. "This is the work of a man who had a vision and

not enough time to work out the nitty-gritty details. It took Einstein a lifetime, and that wasn't long enough. They're still attempting proofs of various parts of the theories, you know. Tyson didn't have a lifetime. He had a few years, three, four. Not enough."

Margaret thought of the garden where Paul had taken her, the hallucination of the garden, she corrected herself hurriedly. "What do you think of what he was doing?" she asked when the silence seemed to be growing too personal somehow.

"I don't know. Yesterday I might have said I thought he was just another crank, but today ... There are hundreds of sects, organizations, study groups, you name it, all searching for this sort of thing. Millions of people have experienced something that has led them to believe that there is a superconsciousness, or heaven, or God-experience, or oceanic feeling, or something, that isn't limited by the space-time laws that we recognize in this reality field that we live in. Every religion, every folklore touches on it sooner or later. It gets stomped to the ground every century—mechanistic man, existential man, electrochemical man—but it never stays down. It's been twisted to fit creeds—the predestination of Calvin and Luther, salvation by good works and prayer, the cyclic theories of limbo until the next cycle begins, reincarnation, with the ultimate aim of unification with the unknowable. ..." He smiled suddenly. "I'm not going to preach to you, Meg. I don't know what I believe yet. Maybe I never will know. I don't believe that man rises from nowhere only to fall back into nowhere after his few years are finished, but where he goes next, I don't know. If he can get there before death, I don't know."

"This . . . this feeling, the mystical experience. Have you had it?" Her hands became very quiet, no longer playing with the pages of the notebook she still held.

"Until yesterday I think I would have said I wasn't certain. Now . . . yes. I know what they mean."

Margaret got up quickly and went to the window. "The sky's on fire. What a strange light." Without turning around she asked, "Why do I feel that I know you? Not just about you. Actually know you. We've never met?" She hadn't meant to ask. She knew the answer.

"I know what you mean. And no, we haven't met before."

She kept her face toward the window. Dawn was hurrying now, streamers of fire stretching from north to south as far as she could see. "Everything's strange out here. Everything's turned topsy-turvy on me. Television. Probably I've seen you on television. Or an article about you."

He didn't reply, and after a moment she turned toward him. "After all," she said rapidly, "you are famous. Many people who meet you probably feel as if they'd known you before."

"Infamous maybe. And you, have you been on television? Or on the cover of *Newsweek?*"

She smiled at the idea. "Of course not."

He continued to regard her steadily. "When you came in here this morning, you weren't surprised to find me already up, were you?" She shook her head. "And as soon as you walked through that doorway, I realized that I had got two cups out, that one of them was ready for you. I wasn't thinking consciously about it, but there it was."

"You were just being polite."

"And you probably noticed that I wasn't sleeping on the

couch as you went by the living room. Our actions just happened to mesh."

He was laughing at her, although no trace showed on his face. "Coincidence," she said, hearing the stiffness in her voice too late.

"Or preview?"

She ignored that as if she hadn't even heard it. She picked up the notebook and when she spoke again, she forced a cooler tone, a more distant and formal hostess voice. "Dr. Bok believes there is a magic place where there is no time as we know it."

"Meg, wait a minute." John reached out and closed his hand over hers on the notebook. "Something else Paul Tyson said once in one of his lectures. I didn't understand it then. He said that development continues long after physical growth stops. Emotional, mental, psychic development goes on and on, but you can deny it and stop along the way. He said it can be frightening sometimes, that it can threaten your entire life, the lives of others. Then you have to choose, quite deliberately."

"You can't choose anything unless you know what the choices are," she said almost hysterically. Not now, she was thinking over and over. Not now. She couldn't think of anything now. Abruptly he released her hand and she sat down. In a rush she said, "Dr. Bok thinks that magic place can be reached. He thinks he can get to it.

"Bok believes that Paul ... Tyson discovered the way. He's very excited by this work. What does he want to use it for? Do you know?"

"Don't you?" John shook his head as if questions were framing themselves that he refused to ask. "I don't know that either. To start a school, to become a latter-day saint who can teach the way, to write a book? Any of those things, I suppose." He stood up then and went to the door looking out. "I wish we didn't have to leave this morning. But I did promise to get them back by noon. I have to go down and see how the boat looks. Do you want to come too?"

They walked without speaking down to the beach. The boat was floating free of the rocks, now restrained only by the anchor. John stared at it in disbelief. It was an old sailboat with an auxiliary engine, painted blue, with orange trim and shining brass fittings. Margaret read the name painted on the side: *La Belle Dame Sans Merci.* She looked again at John Llewellyn, startled. But he was pre-occupied with the problem of reaching the boat, of getting the kids aboard again. He climbed onto the rocks and studied it, then nodded and jumped down again.

"Okay, let's go get the lazyheads up and at it. Clive and Mike can swim out to it from the rocks and lower a boat for the girls." He looked at Margaret apologetically again, "I am sorry we have to leave now. I'd like to stay and talk with you. I want to come back. If the weather holds, would you like to sail on Saturday?"

"Love it," she said.

"Good. I'll come back and anchor and pick you up by noon. Okay?"

The kids were hungry and they ran out of eggs and bacon, and finished the rest of the ham and all the bread and butter. Clive drank a full quart of milk by himself. The girls vanished while the boys went down with John to look over the boat, and when they were all ready to leave, Margaret saw that the girls had cleaned the house. The beds were made, the blankets put away neatly, the bathroom cleaned. She went with them to the beach and stood on the rocks watching as they all got aboard and began to run up the sails, well cleared of the rocks now, with the motor making a steady throbbing sound.

Then there were hands waving and a shout of farewell, and the sails filled and the boat began to move away. Margaret stood on the rocks until it was a speck on the water, and then walked slowly back to the house, feeling very lonely. It was only fifteen after nine when she got back to the kitchen. What could she do all day? She didn't want to see Morris Stein or Bok, and she couldn't bear the thought of remaining inside. She decided to drive to the end of the island, have lunch somewhere along the way, possibly shop a little, for groceries at any rate. As she left the driveway making the turn to the road, she saw Morris Stein appear outside the garage apartment door and stand watching her. He waved for her to stop, or come back, or something and she pretended that she didn't see him. Her heart was pounding, however, and her hands tightened on the steering wheel until she was beyond his line of sight. Why did he affect her like that, she thought angrily. I relaxed a little then; I had got her out of the house, away from Morris Stein for the day, and I needed time to think about him and how to get out from under him. I knew that as soon as he and Margaret were alone again I would be vulnerable, and now I knew too much that I didn't want to tell him. Yet, I would tell him, I suspected. I had no way to defend myself from him. This was the first time that I had been threatened by an outside person in my entire life, and I had to find a way to counter his soothing voice and keep myself intact. What frightened me was the fact that Margaret—I had been able to reach out to John and take him into the void. And that John remembered it. He had said he'd dreamed, but I was certain he remembered and that was why he wanted to come back to talk to Margaret.

Margaret had brought three of the notebooks with her, and she planned to find a quiet beach somewhere, or a deserted restaurant where she would be allowed to sit over coffee and puzzle through them. I knew that if I could get her in the same frame of mind that Morris Stein had brought about, I could make her pore over every page for me, and I would have the time to decipher them even if she couldn't. She turned east, avoiding Baiting Hollow, and then drove steadily, not fast, noticing the scenery, feeling the air on her face. I saw Bok's car almost as soon as he made the turn to the highway, but Margaret didn't notice it. I couldn't see who was driving, but I suspected Morris Stein had been sent after her. Margaret's thoughts had turned to Bennett and Greeley by then, and she was wondering if Bennett would really try to get Greeley to forget that he wanted her to go on the campaign trail with them. She knew that she would not go, regardless of his threats, but how seriously were those threats to be taken? Could he do anything to her father, a high school principal? She didn't think so. It had shaken her badly, having the threat made so openly, so blatantly, and there had been no time to think, but now, she was certain that she could safely ignore him and whatever noises he made.

Margaret began to hum. The farther she got from the house, she was thinking, the clearer and simpler things were becoming for her. Where the tangles had seemed inpenetrable, now they were falling apart by themselves. If she left Bennett, what then? Work again? Probably. And eventually she probably would marry someone else and have children and be busy with P.T.A. and clubs and committees and ... She stopped humming. It didn't have to be like that, she told herself. She would shape her own future, make her life have meaning even if the universe had none.

She was scowling by then and the whole problem of what to do seemed less soluble. She remembered the wholeness she had experienced with Paul in her hallucination and she knew that that was what John Llewellyn had talked about when he said millions experienced something that made them believe in that other dimension. Everything paled in comparison to that one brief illusory experience.

If she could find a way to return to that ... Her hand fell on the notebooks beside her and she began to search for a place to stop.

She had no memory of the several times when it had not been pleasant, when violence and pain had been all too real in the world of illusion. I circled and saw that Morris Stein and Margaret were together talking quietly, then not so quietly. I saw the notebooks open on her knees and read those pages I could see. That might be the way, I decided, and looked for other times when she had finally opened them. Bit by bit I was getting them, a page here, several pages later on; Morris was closing the gap between the two cars, and I had to abandon the notes and watch Margaret. I repeatedly made her notice the rearview mirror and she saw the car coming up without recognition. I gave her a glimpse of the same car parked beside her own on the driveway, and then she realized that she was being followed.

I let her feel my alarm, but it turned her the wrong way. She reacted against it, and instead of running, she decided to stop at the first restaurant she saw and dare him to make a nuisance of himself in a public place. That wasn't the way, I tried to tell her. With four softly spoken words he would have her doing whatever he wanted her to do. I tried to take over and have her outrun him, and even as I did, I knew that there was no place really to run. The road simply ended at the end of the island. She could go so far, and eventually she would have to stop, back up, or make a circle and turn around to go back. There was more ambivalence in Margaret in the next few minutes than she normally would have felt in years. She wanted desperately to be left alone for the day, to think, to read the notebooks, to make decisions. She wanted almost equally desperately to talk to Morris Stein, to tell him about the brief hallucination she had suffered, to talk to him about Paul Tyson and his work. I wanted to talk to him, I knew, and fought that knowledge and the fact, but her foot touched the brake when she saw the sign ahead: *Plum on the Sound—Fine Food.*

Morris was coming in fast now. He wanted to catch up with her before she got inside. I urged her to hurry, made her more afraid, and she almost ran to the door. The restaurant was an old Tudor-design building, with the wood darkened to near black. Inside it was dark and cool, a house converted to a restaurant, very pleasant with chandeliers that were darkened now, but massive and beautiful. There was a long bar, unoccupied, and beyond the arched door, the dining room with three or four tables being used. A man materialized from the dark recess behind the bar.

"One?" he said.

Margaret nodded, glancing toward the door. It was heavy and no sound came through it from the parking lot in front. She followed the man to a table by a window overlooking the sound. He placed a menu before her and withdrew.

One of the tables had three men: lawyers or business-men. A couple, middle-aged, not speaking at all, sat at the second table, and the third one had two middle-aged women who paid no attention to Margaret after her ar-rival, but kept their heads close together talking avidly. Margaret lighted a cigarette and waited. When she heard the door she didn't look up. I heard Morris enter, knew that he stood speaking a moment with the waiter, or whoever he was, and then crossed the floor to Margaret's table.

"Hello, Josie," he said and pulled out a chair.

"Mr. Stein, why did you follow me here? What do you want?"

"Josie, that's not fair. I often come here for lunch. I saw you, it's true, but I thought that you might want to talk to me. Don't you?"

"No," she said tightly.

He laughed and reached across the table to take her hand. "That's not true, is it? You want very much to talk to me. You want to tell me about Paul Tyson and his experiments, don't you?"

I nodded, and Margaret's hand trembled in his. Leave, I told her. Get up and go. Leave your gloves on the table, he'll think you're coming back. Excuse yourself and go. Now. She reached for her purse and started to rise. His hand holding hers tightened and very quietly he said,

"You are very tired, my dear. That's right, sit down, relax. Just sit up normally. But relax. Don't be afraid. In a moment I'm going to tell you to wake up and walk with me to the lounge on the other side of the bar. You'll want to go there with me so we can have a quiet drink and talk a little bit. You won't be afraid at all."

The lounge was very dark, with heavy brown drapes drawn at the windows, and massive green and dark red overstuffed furniture. Margaret sank down into one of the chairs and Morris drew a second one close to hers. He ordered drinks for them both, gin and tonic. The bartender could see them from his place in the bar section of the restaurant, and he looked in now and then and saw only the woman sitting quietly in the deep chair, and the man leaning toward her slightly, sipping his drink, talking peacefully.

Margaret floated and relaxed and I answered questions now and then, not when they were addressed to Josie, but general questions about how I felt, if I was afraid, and things like that. Morris Stein seemed perplexed by something, I noticed, when I noticed him at all, which wasn't often. He said, "Do you remember our lovemaking?"

"Yes."

"You had been very lonesome, hadn't you? You hadn't had it like that for a long time, had you?"

"No."

"You loved Paul Tyson very much, didn't you?"

I was shaken by the question, and I felt myself become more alert, less willing, eager even, to please him. He said, "Relax, relax. That's right." For several minutes he was silent, then he said, "We are going to leave here. I'm going to wake you up and you will eat the sandwich I ordered for you, drink the coffee. You will wake up feeling very good, very relaxed and good. You won't be afraid of me, or try to avoid me. You will drive back to the cottage when we leave here and as soon as you walk inside the house, you will start to remember making love with me. You will remember every detail of it, every little bit of it, and you will find yourself becoming very excited. It will excite you to remember it. You won't want to avoid me ..." He went on several minutes and then woke her up.

Chapter 12

Margaret rationalized returning to the house so early: she
had to have reference books nearby if she was going to
make any sense out of Paul's notebooks; she was very tired
from being up late and rising at dawn; there was no place
where she could count on being left alone anyway, so she
might as well be inside the house. . . .

I was desperately searching through everything I'd ever
read or heard about hypnotism, for a way to escape Morris
Stein. I couldn't find any way to avoid him. I didn't understand how he had done it, why it had worked, but it had,
and as soon as he spoke, I was exposed again. It was as if
Margaret were window dressing only, to be got out of the
way so that he might get directly at me, and she moved
aside obligingly with no memory of having moved at all.
He had given her the verbal concepts of acceptance, of
friendliness, of desire for him, but he couldn't control the
deeper unnamed precepts that also were roused. She
wanted to talk to him, confide in him, and she was afraid
of him at the same time. She felt an unspecified sexual
fascination that she couldn't explain, and yet the thought

of deliberately copulating with him was distasteful to her. What she really wanted was to walk hand in hand with him. Innocently exciting, stimulating, but free of obligation, not involved. Still, she drove toward the house unaware that he was the only reason for her early return.

I was circling, seeing them together again, seeing Bennett with her, Margaret in a canoe with two of her brothers, Josie? Josie and Margaret talking, John's comments to her about Paul Tyson's theories, that he was seeking another point of view of something that seemed nonexistent in itself. Would I be what would survivie if Margaret met a truck head on? Was my existence independent of her entirely, but held to her through ... what? Her aches and pains were nothing to me, never touched me at all. Her wants and needs were not mine. Her appetites were not shared by me. I was pulling farther and farther from her as I wound in and out of these thoughts, and I looked back at her as if from a great distance. She was driving, not as smoothly and surely as usual, but well enough. She was unthinking. As long as I was attached at all, even as tenuously as I was then, she seemed almost normal, but those times I had returned to her from ... that other place, she had been catatonic, kept alive only by that part of her brain that made her heart beat and her lungs and other organs work, that part that never received anything from outside that wasn't first filtered through me. I could take over any of its functions if I chose, but it could do only caretaker work, nothing more. Without me she would have no sensations from outside; there would be no one to sort them out, channel them, understand them. But without her and her sensory capabilities, I could receive nothing else either. This, of course, was the way I could avoid

Morris Stein: I could just leave her when he approached. But could I count on finding my way back to her?

I remembered the lost feeling, and I was certain that so far I had had a guide: Paul. He had helped me find my way back each time. Could I do it alone if I deliberately left her? Could I even cut that last restraining connection at will? I didn't dare try it there with her in the car, but I decided to try as soon as she was alone again. Alone and safely seated, or lying down. I felt almost as if I could turn around and see the way to move to break that tie, but I had no words for it. Another direction, that was the only way I could put words on the idea even to myself.

Margaret saw a sign for a shopping center, two miles to the right, and she made the turn. She was tense, and her compulsion to return to the house directly made her angry and determined to shop first. A pounding headache assailed her as she drove the two miles, and by the time she had finished the short shopping list, she could hardly see, the headache was so pervasive. It began to ease when she turned once more to the highway, but it left a slight throb behind. "I have to go back home," she thought, saying the words. "Straight home again."

She felt a great reluctance to enter the house when she got there. She unloaded the groceries, and put them on the back porch and started to walk toward the steps down to the beach. She felt compelled to go inside the house, and she resisted, her steps slowly faltering until she came to a stop. Finally she turned and walked quickly back to the house, lifted the bag, and went inside.

Imagine an endless corridor with doors lined up into infinity. Usually when she knocked on any of the doors, I could decide whether or not to open it, or how much, whether or not to let her enter, or just hand out a memory to her. This time I could only watch from across a chasm, unable to keep her out, to keep the door closed, to edit or change anything for her. She walked straight in and almost fell on her face at what she saw and felt.

"No," she whispered, closing her eyes hard. "Dear God, no!" But there it was and the harder she tried not to see it, to explain it away as a dream, the clearer the details became: his undressing her on the chair, his hands and his lips on her body, in her body, her cries. She sat down hard, with her eyes still closed and remembered the things he had done to her, remembered her pleasure that had become almost unbearable.

With the returning memories, desire came back also. It was as if he were there doing those things to her again, rousing her again with his lips on her nipples, his fingers at her clitoris. She felt afire and could feel the hardening of her nipples, the upthrust against her bra, could feel the surge of need in her vagina, in her womb, her bowels, a churning that could have been either fear or sexual desire. It was a visitation of an incubus, a being unseen that touched her and played with her body, lingering until each point was raised to a height that could be satisfied only by orgasm; the thought of relief through orgasm made her hug her arms around her body and rock back and forth, with her head bowed, her eyes tightly closed. She couldn't bear this, she thought. When she moved, she felt the chair under her, the pressure on her vulva and she moaned and stood up, looking about almost wildly.

She locked the door and ran to the bedroom, slamming the door behind her, and stood quivering against it. She could feel the heat in her cheeks, and knew that she was flushed, panting, her heart racing hard, and the image of Morris Stein kept rising before her. She shook her head and moaned again. "No no," she whispered. When she raised a hand to her face, it was shaking uncontrollably. She had never felt just like this before, and I was curious about the state of preparedness her body had achieved through a simple suggestion. Often after Bennett's deliberate passion, she was dissatisfied enough to get up and pace, and even masturbate once or twice, but that was after complete arousal by another, not a spontaneous flare-up as this had been. While I watched her, and tried to feel with her the knife edge of desire that was cutting deeper and deeper, I was also considering taboos in general and this one in particular. I couldn't think of her hand groping between her own legs, for instance, without evoking the scene of a small grubby hand feeling the pubic area curiously, a sudden slap, the snatching away of the offensive fingers, the acute distress of her mother. A clear-cut case of conditioning, but there it was, and I tried not to let it rise this time, but it did. Although I didn't let her have that memory, something got through and she was near tears, torn between frustration and need too great to deny. She thought of the first night in the little house: she had tried to bring relief to her aching body then and had failed, but had found a surplus of guilt. I decided to punish Morris Stein. I didn't know how, but there would be a way, and I would find it. Again something got through of my thoughts, and Morris Stein's image presented itself to her and once more she shook her head, with despair this time. She pushed free of the door then, and every motion seemed to increase her sexual tension. She was perspiring, her mouth filled with saliva so that she had to swallow again and again. She was afraid that she was going mad, that she was so deeply sunken in depravity that there was no hope for her. She knew she couldn't stand this, and she began to tear off her clothes. Shower, she thought. Long. Cool. Stinging. Shower. She left clothing strewn behind her and went into the bathroom and saw her reflection in the full-length mirror, nipples upright, hard, a high red flush on her cheeks, sensitive to the touch of her own arms as they brushed her body, the feel of nylons as she stripped off her stockings. She reached behind her to release the hooks of the garter belt, and she brushed the down on her buttocks and suddenly was shaking all over. Raising her gaze once more to her reflection, she touched one of her hard, sore-looking nipples, and suddenly her hands were as brutal as Morris Stein's had been. She pressed one breast hard, squeezing it against her ribs, and her other hand clutched the mound that seemed to jump up to meet the unsteady fingers. She backed into the seat of the toilet and sat down on the edge of it, spreading her legs wide apart, and, tentatively at first, then harder and harder, she thrust her fingers inside her vagina as far as she could, and wished she had something she could use, it wasn't enough, she couldn't reach enough, she wanted to hurt herself, to be filled to choking. Her other hand left the nipple to rub savagely at the clitoris and she felt the welling, the fire raging now, and at last the final climax ripped through her, and with a sobbing cry she felt her convulsive orgasm, and the hot flow of fluid scalded her hand. She jerked it free, and fell to her knees, with her head cradled on her arms on the side of the bathtub, and she sobbed and wept, her body heaving with the violence of her reaction for many minutes.

She pushed herself up and away from the support of the tub and turned on the shower and stood under it for ten minutes, trying not to think, not touching herself, simply letting water sting her body and cleanse it once more. She hadn't heard either of the two cars screech to a stop at the driveway, then enter, too fast for the rough conditions of the deteriorated expanse. The first one I had recognized as Bok's car, and I wondered where Morris Stein had been, what had delayed him. This isn't what he'd had in mind for Margaret, I knew. I wondered if he had become frantic with worry over her, not knowing how the memories would have affected her, not being there to reap the benefits. I'll get you, Morris Stein, I said again. The second car, which followed his by minutes, was one I didn't know, and now with the shower turned on as hard as it would go, I wasn't able to hear anything at all from outside the closure.

When Margaret at last turned off the water and began to towel herself, she knew that it wasn't over yet. As soon as the towel brushed across her breast, the nipple hardened again, and the desire that she had thought banished returned. She bit her lip and dried herself roughly, and went into the bedroom naked, to find clothes.

I heard the man moving about in the living room seconds before he walked far enough for me to recognize his steps as Bennett's. When Margaret first heard movement, she thought it was Morris Stein. At once she was back at the moment of greatest need of sexual relief, and she ran to the door and stood leaning against it weakly, wanting to throw it open and go to him, wanting equally as much to lock it and wait for him to go away.

"Margaret, are you finished yet?"

She almost fell. Bennett! Hurriedly she pulled on her robe and went into the living room.

"Bennett, what's the matter? Is something wrong?"

"I should ask you that. I called and called, first it was busy, then no answer. Where've you been?"

They stood on opposite sides of the room hurling questions at each other, and both fell silent at the same moment. Margaret shrugged and turned first, going into the kitchen. She said over her shoulder, "I went shopping. I was gritty, so I showered before putting the things away. Do you want a sandwich or something?"

"No." He followed her and watched as she emptied the bag. His gaze kept returning to her face, and he said abruptly, "Margaret, stop all that. Sit down a minute. Why did you have the phone off the hook?"

She sat down by him at the small kitchen table. "I found it off at about ten," she said, "and put it back. I must have knocked it off earlier without noticing. And today I drove awhile, then shopped and came home." She felt momentarily that she was leaving something out, but whatever it was, it was gone, and she waited.

Bennett suddenly stood up and went to the door, making certain it was locked. "Do those two come right in when they get ready? I saw the kid starting to come up the back stoop when I drove up. He saw me and left. What are they doing?"

"I don't really know. Research into the work of Paul Tyson. I will let them take out only one notebook at a time, and when they finish it and bring it back, I give them another one. They're working in the apartment over the garage."

He wasn't really listening. He looked at her again, and

quickly averted his gaze. "I feel such a fool," he said after a moment. "I never had a suspicious moment before, not until Arnold Greeley planted the idea. But now, with you, I feel like an idiot. Have you been crying?"

"Soap," she said.

He nodded. "You . . . you're looking very beautiful. And you act differently somehow. You're not ... I mean, Margaret, are you pregnant?"

She was startled at the thought and shook her head. Bennett came up to her and touched her cheek lightly. She didn't move away, but he passed on behind her chair and, standing behind her, his hand caressed her neck, then slid down her robe and inside it. He stopped when his fingers came in contact with her nipple that was still hard and upright. His hand tightened and his other hand on her shoulder dug in hard. He squeezed her breast, hurting her, then withdrew his hand and said, in a thick, almost unrecognizable voice, "Get dressed. I'll take you to an early dinner down in Hampstead. I know a nice place. We'll come home early and get some sleep. And in the morning I have to catch a flight back down to Atlantic City."

Margaret felt the blood suffuse her face and neck at his touch, then drain away, leaving her almost faint. She stood up unsteadily, and turned toward him. "Bennett . . ." She was holding the chair back to keep her balance. If he would take her now, she knew there would be an end to so many things. If only he would learn her sexuality, her needs that were as great, as bad, she thought first, as his own, or even more powerful maybe than his. Take me to bed and make me come again and again and again, she cried silently. Please, Bennett.

He turned from her and said, "Is there any Scotch

left?" Before she could speak, he had found it, and he said, "For God's sake, go get dressed. One of those men could come up here any minute and look right in and see you."

"Bennett, let's not go out to dinner now. It's early." Her voice sounded like a stranger's to her ears.

He had poured a drink by then and finally turned around to face her. His face was a mask. "If I touch you right now, I'll treat you like one of the dirtiest whores I've ever had."

She was looking at his hand clutching a glass. Long, strong fingers she was thinking. They would be good. His voice jolted her.

"I almost beat the last whore I had to death," he said thickly. "Do you know what I'm saying to you? She was a filthy degenerate, and I almost beat her to death before I took her." He took a long swallow. "Sometimes you remind me of her, or someone else a long time ago that was like her. Then I become ashamed. You are so good, so innocent. It frightens me when I suddenly see you like that. I know it's me, in me. A devil in me. . . ." He stopped, and Margaret turned and left the kitchen without speaking.

As soon as Margaret left the house the enchantment ended. I felt it leave first, and the hurdle that had been between her and me was gone, we were united again. I hadn't realized just how dispossessed I had been by the enactment of the suggestion, but as long as she had been laboring under it, I had been an outsider almost, and now I was one with her, or as much a unity as we ever were. She felt it as a lessening of tension, a sudden give, a release that felt as though a constricting band had been cut from around her chest. She took a deep breath and closed her eyes briefly before exhaling again. Bennett looked at her quickly, but said nothing, and she didn't explain.

She thought of the strange scene played between them, and considered his words over and over. How could she have begged, well, practically begged, the way she had done? She had no desire for him whatever now; it was as cold and dead as she had come to expect it to be with him. She didn't even want him to take her when they returned to the house. Perhaps tonight would be the time to tell him they were finished. She frowned and lighted a cigarette and tried to form the words and sentences that she would need to get through that scene. Scenario: living room. Decidedly not the bedroom. Not the kitchen, she might be provoked and throw something, and that would be bad. She hadn't thrown anything at anyone since ... twelve, thirteen? She couldn't remember. I did. A pottery bowl at her oldest brother. He had ducked, taunting her to try again, and she had, with a hand-painted fruit dish that had caught him in the solar plexus, completely winding him, knocking him down. Margaret remembered only that she had hit him and he had fallen down. And her contrition. She hadn't thrown anything since. But she had a strong compulsion against arguing in the kitchen.

Bennett asked her what she did all day and night, alone in the house. She didn't hear him and he repeated it, with an edge on his voice.

"I've been alone remarkably little, as a matter of fact," she said. When she told him about the shipwreck and the overnight guests, he frankly didn't believe her.

"Okay," he said after the story, "I asked for that. I wasn't prying."

"What do you mean?"

"You don't have to make up stories for my benefit."

"It happened. What in the world do you think I'd invent it for?"

"I don't know. But, Margaret, a sailing boat wouldn't happen to come onto the only outcropping of rocks along that stretch, then free itself overnight. And obviously if there had been five extra people in the house there would be signs of it today. Let's drop it." There was a trace of bitterness in his tone, and she knew that the doubts that Arnold Greeley had planted in him were not still rootless. She shrugged and turned her attention to the countryside, but she didn't really see it.

I was just barely hanging on. Margaret was drowsy and didn't need anything, so I left her alone and paid attention to other things: the changing light as the sun went down farther nad farther, darkening shadows, stretching them. I went over the union with John Llewellyn, the merger of two into one that had been so satisfying, more so than any of the brief touches that sexual intercourse occasionally provided. I looked at Margaret from my great distance and yearned for her, just as she often yearned for me, and neither of us could be fulfilled until that yearning was satisfied, I knew, but didn't know how to bring it about. It was as if all doors opened one way, and I couldn't budge them from my direction, and she was afraid to try from hers.

The drive was silent. When they went into the nice restaurant Bennett felt that he had to make conversation in order not to appear gauche. He dreaded public silences. Margaret looked as though she was listening, although, actually, she paid very little attention to his words.

Dinner was mediocre, the service rather poor, and Bennett was in a bad mood by the time they left. I suspected that he was wishing they had stayed in Josie's house, and with the coming of dusk that he had jumped Margaret in bed. He had that look.

The cooler Margaret became, the more his tension increased on the way home. He wanted her to sit closer, and she pretended to be afraid of the road with a one-armed driver. He began to talk about how lovely she had looked when he got to the house that noon, and she said primly, thank you, and turned on the radio, too loud. The news came on at nine, then a weather forecast of fog and mild temperatures through Friday night. She hoped Saturday would be clear and warm, with a brisk wind, a good sailing wind.

And I worried about the limitations of suggestion Morris Stein had given her. Would she go into a passionate trance when she reentered the house? She had forgotten again the night of lust spent with Morris Stein, and that seemed rather unpredictable of her, unexpected. I was almost certain that he had meant for her to continue to remember that scene, but I could not serve it up unless she tried to get it. Some of my preoccupation with this filtered through to her, so that by the time Bennett parked the car outside the house, she had a feeling of unease, but baseless and general rather than specific. When she walked into the house, no trigger was pulled. It was over. She felt curiously gay then and again could find no reason for it. Bennett, following her, locked the door after glancing toward the apartment over the garage, muttering something about too many people around.

Margaret went into the living room, turning on every

lamp as she passed it, and finally settling down on the couch with a book. Bennett stood in the doorway loosening his tie. "Why don't you go ahead and get ready for bed," he said lightly. "I'll be in in a minute."

Margaret didn't look up. "I really don't think I'm quite ready yet, dear. You get some sleep."

Bennett's script had two different exit lines for bedtime. One was: "Goodnight, dear. I'm ready, I guess." *Exit.* The other: "Why don't you go ahead and get ready for bed. I'll be in in a minute." *Exit Margaret.* After the first week of marriage, Margaret never had missed a cue until that night. I was in close, interested, curious, responsible, probably, for the increase in the adrenaline that spurted through her.

If he will only, please, not be reasonable with me, Margaret thought. Bennett stood undecided in the dorway, then came into the living room and sat in the chair opposite her. He was going to be reasonable. Margaret thought: if he would come over here and demonstrate, show me what he wants, make me want it too. . . .

Bennett said, "What is it, Margaret? Tell me what I've done."

She looked up wide-eyed. "You've done? What do you mean?"

"You know. When I came in today, you were ... anxious almost. You wanted to make love then. What happened?"

"Oh, how can you ask what happened? I felt ... I wanted you. Now I don't feel in the mood at all. Why do I need a reason? You never need a reason. You either do or you don't, no explanation."

He looked shocked. I was delighted. She seldom managed to shock him. Go, girl, go, I urged her, but she ignored me and suddenly felt ashamed. I increased the adrenaline again and her anger returned.

"For God's sake, Margaret! You can't compare us like that. You know that's not fair. I'm sorry about today. You surprised me. I'd never seen you so ... ready. Anyway, I want to make it up to you. I am truly sorry."

Margaret stood up, her cheeks flaming, but with anger this time, not passion. She said deliberately, "I want you to watch me undress, watch us in the act of intercourse, see our bodies together, not act like it's something dirty. Can you do that? Can you prolong it for my benefit? Let me come more than once, a dozen times if that's what I want? Can you treat me like another person who wants satisfaction, instead of like an object designed only to receive your penis and your semen?"

Margaret blinked hard. Bennett was mixing a drink in the kitchen. She recalled her words and knew she couldn't do that. It wouldn't go like that anyway. She couldn't bring herself to say such things to him.

Margaret rejected the scene. She didn't want him to talk to her. She wanted his passion to match what he believed it to be. She wanted him to discover that she too had passion, which he had ignored for so many years. She stood up and looked about undecided, then went into the bedroom and undressed. She searched through Josie's clothing and brought out a filmy peignoir and a pale pink sash that tied just under her breasts. She put on nothing under it and looked at herself in the mirror before she returned to the living room. Her nipples, the light brown pubic hair, the dimple that was her navel, her buttocks, and the long gash between them, nothing was hidden under the garment, only misted over slightly. She loosened her hair and let it fall about her shoulders and left the bedroom.

Bennett stared at her for a moment, then quickly drank the Scotch and water that he had prepared. "Why don't you go ahead and get ready for bed. I'll be in in a minute." Margaret stifled a giggle and returned to the bedroom.

Get ready for bed? She was ready. She dropped the peignoir on the floor, pulled the spread and covers from the bed and lay on the pale cool sheets naked, at the last moment crossing her legs and putting her hands under her head. Now.

She listened to the bathroom noises, grew uncomfortable and had to put her arms down to her sides and uncross her legs to stretch. She was very tired, after all, and the thought of sleeping rather than lovemaking was very attractive. When she heard him at the door, she quickly resumed her pose. Bennett entered, dressed in his robe, and drew up sharply when he saw her. He pulled off his glasses and Margaret knew that immediately she became a blur to him. Somewhere deep inside her I started to laugh, and she heard it, recognized it, and let a slight smile curve her lips. She watched Bennett cross the room and turn off the light, heard him stumble over a chair, and my laughter almost escaped her lips.

Bennett sat on the side of the bed to take off his slippers and his pajamas. He folded them, was momentarily puzzled about where to put them because of the tumble of bedclothing at the foot of the bed and floor, and finally added them to the heap. Then he lay down next to her, on his left side, and his right hand reached for her.

She found herself counting: one, two, three, four. One, two, three, four. The nipple hardened under his thumb and forefinger and he left it to take the left one. It was more awkward to reach somehow, and there was no contact at all between them except for his hand at her breast. One, two, three, four. One ... It hardened. His hand slid down her body. He shifted and his mouth came down on her mouth, as if to distract her attention from what his hand was doing. One, two, three. ... The clitoris was more sensitive than she could remember its ever being before. If only his lips weren't so thick, so wet. He sucked at her mouth and his fingers pressed the tiny upright bit of flesh this way and that until she felt her hips moving, her legs opening. He touched the mouth of her vagina very briefly, only to see if it was ready, and then shifted again, this time throwing his leg over her, squashing her momentarily until he could get his weight on his elbows. He guided the penis in carefully and she surged toward him uncontrollably. He grunted and plunged. And again. She heard the faintly mocking cadence being counted: one, two ... No! she thought. Stop it. Go to him, let it happen. Show him how it can be, what he's been missing, making you miss.

He said, "Did you come?"

She shook her head, blinded by sudden, unexpected tears. He plunged again and then again and again. She tried to move her legs, to bring them up, and he shifted his body slightly, keeping her flat, her legs widespread and flat against the bed. One, two, three, four. It was coming, she thought, now, welling, swelling, filling, thrilling. ... Don't stop, she wanted to cry, please, don't stop now, harder and harder now, there and there, near the top. No, no, not deeper, near the top. Please, don't ... She came then, suddenly, quickly, intensely, too briefly. He stopped all motion for several seconds, still refused to allow her to lift her legs, and when she was finished he started a different rhythm, long strokes that were more exciting than the ones he thought she required. She tried to shift under him and couldn't.

"Bennett, don't come yet. Not yet." He laughed and his strokes became harder, his grunts deeper.

She knew it would be over in seconds. Suddenly she saw him, grunting, humping, intent. She wanted to laugh, but her excitement was growing again, climbing again, rising to meet him, contracting, trying to draw him in farther, rising. There, she wanted to cry. Do me there! He had no thoughts of her then, strokes deep and hard and fast, she was climbing faster, could feel it coming up, again welling, harder this time, more responsive, more demanding. ... He came with a loud groan and fell down on her and it was over.

She felt choked with disappointment, stifled by his weight, used merchandise. The phrase came unbidden and with it came tears. If he knew she wept he made no mention of it, but after a moment rolled off her, and got up and went into the bathroom, taking his robe and pajamas with him. She heard running water, heard the toilet flush, then silence as he dressed for bed. She got up and pulled on her own warm fuzzy robe and slippers. She wiped herself with Kleenex, feeling nothing but distaste for the stickiness between her legs. She didn't fix the bedclothes.

When Bennett came back to the bedroom, she was sitting down smoking a cigarette. "Not sleepy yet?" he asked. He didn't look directly at her.

"We have to talk," she said.

"Now?"

"Now. I want to leave you."

"Darling! That isn't funny." He heaved the blanket and top sheet from the floor and tossed them onto the bed. He had them so twisted that he would never get it made unless he separated out the various parts first. He was trying to smooth them down together.

"I don't think it's funny either," Margaret said, watching him fumble with the cover. "Take off the blanket and do the sheet first," she said after a moment.

He ignored her suggestion and tried to pull the sheet straight without removing the blanket. The mass ended up half on the bed, half on the floor, with a corner in the exact center of the bottom sheet.

"Because of Arnold Greeley? Is that still bothering you?"

"I could say that's it, but it would be a lie. If you keep tugging at them together, you'll never get them both on the bed. Static electricity is holding them together."

He scowled at her and walked around the bed, carrying the corner of the top sheet in his hand, with the blanket trailing over it also. It was the top corner of the blanket, joined with the lower corner of the sheet, that he tucked under the mattress, making the blanket look like a triangular-shaped splash of yellow with one corner missing. He found it on the floor and stood holding it, perplexed.

"Oh, for heaven's sake." Margaret said. She put down her cigarette and yanked the blanket from him. She pulled it free of the sheet, making sparks jump, and tossed it to the floor. Then she arranged the sheet quickly, pulled the blanket back in place and tucked it in.

"Margaret, you can see how much I need you. I told you I could take care of Arnold Greeley, that you wouldn't be bothered any more by him. I promise. Please let's both go back home tomorrow and get back to a normal life. . . ."

"Bennett," she said, using the same pleading tone that he had used, "you can see how tired I am of you. You need me like you need a part-time job. There's absolutely nothing I can do or give you that you can't hire done, or buy. Nothing."

"How can you say that after tonight? I love you. I know that you love me. Darling, I know what the problem is. I've discussed it with Dr. Schloss. He said I could expect you to become restless if you didn't conceive, but Dr. Crellen has the answer to that. You're taking the pills, and in a few more months when you stop, just wait and see. You'll blossom like the desert after a rain."

She laughed then. She couldn't help herself. "Stop," she said helplessly, tears streaming down her cheeks, when he tried to take her in his arms. "That's so funny. You really want to believe, want to make me believe it's my fault, don't you? You, an only child of an only child."

"My father wasn't an only child. You forgot about Josie."

"And whose child was Josie? Are you certain about her?" Bennett was jolted backward by her words. Before he could recover, she went on, "How dare you talk to my doctor about me! How dare you talk to a psychiatrist about me! I've never consulted your Dr. Schloss and you know it. How dare he make a diagnosis of me from a distance! Have you ever had your own sperm tested for fertility? Have you dared?"

Bennett was very pale and agitated. "I told you when I wanted you tested that I had. You know that."

"I know what you told me, but I don't believe you. You are sterile. Why won't you admit it and adopt a child? You're not fooling anyone but yourself. Your father's line is run out."

"Shut up! Don't say that!"

"Admit it. Adopt a child!"

"Dr. Schloss said you might not be able to face up to the knowledge of your barrenness. You have to go see him next week. I'll make the appointment. ... I told him you were becoming frigid, so you needn't be ashamed to talk freely to him."

"You told him ..." She laughed again, more wildly than before.

"Margaret, please stop. You're becoming hysterical. Have you any sleeping pills left?"

"Frigid," she gasped. "Bennett, let me tell you why I'm leaving." He hurriedly left the bedroom and returned in a moment with two pink capsules and a glass of water.

"Just swallow them, dear. We'll talk in the morning."

She threw the capsules in his face, snatched the glass from him and dashed the water after the capsules. He backed from her, blinded without his glasses, trying to dry them on a handkerchief that was also wet.

"You are willfully blinding yourself, aren't you?" she cried. "You are doing this deliberately! You are using me, hoping I'll bear your child, using me like a plot of ground that you keep tossing dead seeds on. But you've got to plow that ground, Bennett, and take care of it. You treat your whores better than you do me. You treat them like women!"

"Margaret, stop. You're screaming. You'll have Bok and that kid in here. Calm yourself."

"Why don't you realize that I'm a woman too. I want to fuck, to have the satisfaction of being used up completely, wholly, with nothing left for the sailors and soldiers. . . ."

Bennett turned and ran out, and she threw an ashtray at him as he went through the doorway, spilling cigarette butts and ashes across the room.

Margaret sat straight up in the chair. Bennett came back from the bathroom and smiled at her and then fell into bed, pulling up the cover and sheet with one movement. She stared at him. He turned on his side and sighed, and slowly she turned off the light and walked from the bedroom. He didn't ask if she was coming to bed now. Moments later as she paced the living room, I heard the first rumble of a snore.

Chapter 13

Margaret vaguely remembered making the fire in the living room, but she had no memory of lying down on the couch, of dozing there all night. Toward dawn I found it again.

I stopped, feeling it just ahead of me, a turn in direction away. It waited as I paused. She was all right. There was no reason for the hesitation, but I stopped. I felt ahead cautiously; there was no discernible barrier, and no way to anticipate the exact moment when I would no longer be bound to Margaret and inside the other place again. I never had been able to consider before. This time it was as if I were being given the choice: to enter, or to stay outside. Why? I searched for a presence, anything, and I knew that whatever it was, I would find it only after making the decision, after going through.

There was a shift, then I was in a room that was sunlit and bright, with pots of scarlet blooming plants, and tall wide-open windows beyond which were fields and forests. There was the sound of a surf nearby, and perfumed air, sweet with summer blossoms, alive with birdsong and the hum of insects. A man and a woman were in the room. If they had been there from the beginning, I had been blind to them, but there they were. I knew it was Paul and Josie. I felt no disappointment, only joy to be there. Josie took my hand and led me on into another room, a sun porch with wicker furniture and blue-green flooring. Although I knew she was lovely, when I turned away from her I couldn't describe her at all, except that she was enchanting.

Paul brought a tray with glasses of lemon-tasting drinks and it was nothing that I had ever had before. Everything was strange yet familiar, new yet accustomed. I had been there always, would be there always, this was all of life and sufficient.

Paul said, not in words, but in my brain, "We'll teach it all to you and you will be able to use it whenever you want to."

I soared and was not alone now. The circles were greater than ever, and I merged now with Paul, now with Josie, and there were no secrets between any of us. I learned the direction I had to turn, and how to turn again to go back to Margaret. I could remember Margaret dimly and I knew I never would go back to her unless they forced me to; I had been there always, everything else was a sham, a make-believe world. Josie shared my thoughts and she surrounded me with her love, and under it I sensed her sadness for me and knew that I couldn't remain there. For some reason that I didn't comprehend I wasn't ready, couldn't be taken in and kept. I probed them both and understanding came but not acceptance.

I would not be responsible for Margaret. I hadn't asked for her, didn't need her, didn't want her. I hated her intensely, and this drove Josie and Paul farther from me. I thought of Margaret, that shadowy creature of lusts and wants and contradictory drives and fears, and I rejected her completely. I would refuse to return, I said to them, circling in narrowing arcs now.

"You did refuse to go back," Paul said.

I felt only confusion. "I don't know what you mean."

"I know. But you will."

Josie withdrew first. She stood by a glass-topped table and smiled at Paul, then touched his cheek lightly and began to fade. I stared until she was gone. Paul's face showed no surprise, no regret.

"Where is she?"

"She went back. She had to go back. Just as you do."

"But you don't even care. You could keep her."

He shook his head. "Not yet."

"And you said I refused to go back. When? I don't understand." I felt myself standing also then and looked about. The house was shimmery, and a blue mist was settling over the distant forests, swirling gently in the fields. "I didn't have a choice before. I never knew what this was, where I was. It all just happened to me. The first time it happened, I was so frightened. . . ."

"This is the first time," he said, smiling now. "You have to think about it, Meg. You have all the answers now, all of them. Not through the intellect, but through our help, your own intuition. Now you have to think." He touched me, as Josie had touched him, lightly, lingeringly, on the cheek, and his touch became ephemeral, a whisper of warm air, then nothing. I turned around and returned to Margaret.

She stirred slightly, adjusted her position, and went back

to sleep on the couch where Bennett found her in the morning. She was very hard to awaken; I had to come from a long way away before she really heard him. I knew a lot of what Paul and Josie had found by then, but it was without words.

"Margaret! Wake up!" Bennett wasn't actually shaking her; he had her arm and was waving it up and down ineffectually.

"Bennett, stop ... I'm awake. I ... I was dreaming, I think." She sat up and faintly remembered sitting down to watch the fire. It had burned out. I was impatient for Bennett to go away. I knew that I had to force Margaret to look inside herself, and it wouldn't be easy, but it was necessary. I couldn't begin with Bennett there. She felt some of this, enough to want him to go catch his plane. She got up and made coffee while he finished dressing and getting ready. She scrambled eggs for him and squeezed oranges and made toast. She was feeling very strange, not dopey as she did after sleeping pills, but dissociated somehow, not completely there with Bennett. He was in a jovial mood now.

"I'll be back Sunday," he said munching toast and strawberry jam. "With that littlt airport down in Hampstead, I can fly back several times a week, much easier actually than back to the apartment."

She nodded and sipped her coffee. It was so hard to imagine his getting all involved with someone like Arnold Greeley, politics. She said suddenly, "Bennett, why are you in this? What do you want from it?"

"What do you mean?" He was immediately defensive.

"I'm not picking a fight. I'm curious, that's all. What will you gain?"

"Oh. Notice, maybe. I think Greeley is going to shake things up rather a lot. I have ideas, you know. He can implement them."

She nodded. He didn't know. He hadn't made the choice any more than she had chosen anything most of her life. And her? He hadn't chosen her, not Margaret Fowler the woman, but he had been chosen, had gone along with the idea of marrying Margaret Fowler, sister of four boys, with three uncles on her mother's side of the family, and four on her father's side. What were the odds on her conceiving and bearing a male child? She didn't know, but she suspected that he did. If she had been cross-eyed, homely, stupid . . . Any number of things probably would have disqualified her, but she ticked off a mental list that he must have had in mind and found that the major disadvantages were really only money and social position, and he had been able to fix them for her. She smiled and he thought she was smiling approval.

"I'm glad I came back," he said. "I discovered a new facet of you, and that's pleasant. When I saw how passionate you were yesterday I was startled. You have been so controlled all the time. It pleases me that my unexpected arrival can do that to you."

She almost laughed.

Bennett finished his coffee and stood up. He kissed her cheek, checked his keys for the rented car, got his coat and the briefcase that had become a part of him since his preoccupation with Arnold Greeley, then left. "Until Sunday," he said at the door. "I'll bring you a pretty."

She nodded. Morris Stein would be watching, I knew, and as soon as he realized she was alone, we could expect him to call. What to do about him? Margaret had another cup of coffee in the living room, with the kitchen door bolted against intrusion and tried to think rationally about Morris Stein. She didn't want to see him, and still, there was something that had to be done, something that had to be said ... she didn't know what it was. I waited until she put down her cup, and then I made the turn and stepped into the void. It was that easy.

I didn't stay. I had wanted only to test it, and it worked. Margaret had a feeling of momentary amnesia; and she had forgotten what she had been thinking about. I didn't know if I could wait for him to try to get control before leaving her; I wasn't at all certain it would work after his magic words had been said. On the other hand, I didn't dare not wait.

He came about fifteen minutes later. Margaret tried to ignore the pounding on the door, but the mixed feelings that assailed her finally led her to the kitchen and she admitted him.

"Josie, are you all right?"

"Of course. Do you want another notebook?"

"No. I want to talk to you. You were going to tell me about Paul, his work, his experiments, findings, remember?" He laughed in embarrassment and said, "Yesterday a cop nabbed me for speeding, held me up." Probably nothing else could have kept him away. Slowly I nodded. I had an overwhelming impulse to tell him all about the void, all I had learned. At the same time I knew that if he went there, he might never get back without a guide, and I couldn't be his guide. I nodded again. "Coffee?" Margaret said. "Sit down."

Morris Stein sat at the kitchen table and watched her as

she got a cup out and filled it. He added cream and sugar, and then waited.

"It's another dimension," I said, and knew that Margaret would remember none of this. I tried to rouse her, to bring her back in, but she had sidestepped again, and I had to talk through her.

"I know. How do you reach it? What's there?"

"You have to be taught how. If you stumble in inadvertently you can be lost, never to find your way out again, or be seized by someone already there. You have to be taken in at first, taught how, and then you can go alone." For a moment I almost remembered something I had planned to do when he arrived, but it was gone quickly, and I waited for him to ask another question.

"Josie, have you been there? You know the way?"

Josie? I felt momentarily confused, and with the brief respite the spell was broken. I turned and left. I was content for a period not to have anything about me, no break in the gray, but then it became oppressive, the absence of everything made nothing too threatening, and I brought in light and form. A room with a window, a lamp, desk ... it was very like Paul's room. I said to myself that when I looked through the window, I would be able to see Margaret and Morris Stein through it. I was there instantly, and it was as if I had a view of the kitchen from a point that was at once inside it, and still removed so that I could see every spot simultaneously. Morris Stein was feeling Margaret's pulse. He released her wrist and opened first one eye, then the other to peer at the whites. He stood up and stared at her motionless figure, one hand slightly raised where he had left it, and he reached and took the hand and placed it in her lap. Then he left the house. I went back to Margaret.

She was frightened this time. She remembered that Morris Stein had knocked, that she had admitted him, then nothing. I knew that I had to have her to myself now, that I had to make the breakthrough or she might crack up so thoroughly that they would hospitalize her, and with sedation and drugs make her wholly inaccessible to me. First, the door. She bolted it just as Morris Stein and Bok appeared at the garage steps. She watched them hurry toward the house and then went into Paul's room and closed that door so that she would be farther from the pounding that would erupt on the back door. She sat in Paul's chair, afraid and miserable.

It was the house, she decided. She never had believed in haunted houses before, but this one must be haunted by Paul's ghost. She had changed into a stranger since arriving here. All the sexual preoccupation, the dream-heavy sleep, the blackouts. . . . She was really losing her mind. It was as if, by adopting Josie's name, pretending, she had opened herself to possession, until now she no longer knew who she was, why she was there. She heard Morris Stein calling Josie's name at the windows, and she pressed her hands over her ears. She was Margaret. Meg. Darling Meg. No! That was part of the madness. But John Llewellyn called her Meg, too. Was he real? Were the kids real, the girl with the white hair? Something stirred within her as the memory of the girl with the white hair touched a nerve, and she shied away from the memory. She didn't know if they had been real or not. She didn't know if Bok was real, or Morris Stein. Had she walked with her hand in his? Why did she respond in her groins to the sound of his voice? Why did she fantasize about opening her legs to him, about having his mouth on hers, on her breasts. And, oh, God, his mouth at her clitoris.

She stood up, her hands still tight on her ears. She would tell them the truth, tell them she had hoaxed them, and they would go away. But ... had Bok really undressed her, had she pleaded with him to take her? She didn't know. She threw herself across Paul's bed. Would they break down a door, force a lock? Why didn't they just take the notebooks and leave her alone? What did they want from her?

I knew they were outside the kitchen door again, listening, waiting for her to open the door for them. I could hear their whispering voices, but not the words. Bok was furious with Morris Stein. I forced Margaret to get up and go to the door to listen, and I knew that she had to show herself, or call out, or something. They were afraid she had gone into a catatonic state again.

They would force their way in if she didn't show herself soon in a fairly normal manner. I was thinking furiously. There had to be a way to face Morris Stein, to erase her fear and longing for him. Margaret was weaker than I, I knew that. The external Margaret was almost mindless, if untouchable. I wouldn't let her order me about. Why did I let Morris Stein do it? It was as if she moved over and let him take her place, but her place then became my place. It was curious. When she said, with determination, "I will remember," it didn't mean that I would hand out the memory for her. Some memories were tied up with others that would be too traumatic for her to handle; others were simply hard to find when wanted; some were rejected by her as soon as I served them up, rejected, repressed again, but by her, not me. If only that door weren't a one-way door, I thought bitterly. If I could force it open, make her see what she had to see. If only she would realize what he could do to her, and refuse to move over. I thought about that. The physical changes that came over her: the initial flurry of her heart, anticipation and fear mostly; the relaxation that followed, letting the third part of her brain take over complete control of the muscles with no supervision at all. I felt that I was getting away from the center of the problem. When she moved over, why was he able to take control of me? That was the issue.

Bok's voice came through then. "Josie, my dear. Please open the door. I am worried about you. We'll have to force it if you won't open. Are you all right?"

Margaret bit a knuckle and moved toward the kitchen door. They would get inside if they really wanted to. She went to the door and stood to one side of it. "Go away, Dr. Bok. Just go away and leave me alone."

"Josie, you are very tir ..."

I made her forget the words as they formed, as she heard them. She felt a stir of something, but it left quickly and she waited for them to leave.

"Josie, open the door." Morris Stein's voice.

She shook her head. "Go away, both of you."

He tried it again, and this time it was easier. I knew how to thwart him now. He was no longer a threat. Margaret felt the relief too, and when she shrugged and started to unlock the door, I didn't even try to prevent it. I was feeling jubilant.

As soon as the door opened, Morris Stein pushed in ahead of Bok. He said, "Sit down, Josie. Sit down and relax."

She stared at him, then turned puzzled eyes on Bok. "Are you almost finished with the material yet?" she asked. "This is getting to be rather a nuisance, you know. I haven't had an hour alone since I came here for a rest."

Bok glared at Morris Stein, who looked at Margaret with disbelief. He opened his mouth, then shut it tightly without uttering a word. I wished I could laugh. Margaret was merely puzzled by him.

Bok said to Margaret, "If you would only help us a little, it would go so much faster, my dear. I know it's an ordeal for you, but there is so much that is not plain in the notes, so much that you know personally that we are having to work over and rework."

Margaret sighed. Without knowing where the information was coming from, whether she had read it in the letters, or dreamed it, or was making it up as she spoke, she said, "Paul nearly died, you know." Bok shook his head, and she smiled. "Yes, he did. They said officially that it was a very minor heart attack, from which he fully recovered, but that was wrong. He nearly died, or perhaps did die briefly. He wasn't certain himself. His work in physics had led him to know that on the subatomic level, at the pure energy level, time doesn't exist, not the linear time that we know. During his illness, especially when the heart attack struck, he experienced this same timelessness that he had observed in the laboratory on a macrocosmic scale, not merely the microscopic. He knew that it was more important than continuing his work at Brookhaven, and further, that it was not the sort of experimental work that he could justify to his director, so he resigned. You have the results of his theoretical work, his mathematics, his proofs. I know nothing about any of that. He guided me all the way, and without him, without someone who knows the way you have to duplicate what he did. But first, you have to know that it is possible." She smiled gently at Bok. "First comes faith, then the evidence, you see. The effects of experimenter bias are of the greatest importance in this area."

Morris Stein had been listening attentively, but now he turned aside angrily and said, "I knew it. Auto-conditioning; deep trance state that reinforces the original belief constitutes proof. Garbage."

Bok paid no attention to him. Eagerly he said to Margaret, "But he did show you how, didn't he? You can do it? You did it a while ago when Morris was questioning you, didn't you?"

She smiled and said, "I don't know what you're talking about."

"He showed you the way! Don't deny it. It's in all the notes. It's in your face. You have the skin and body of a very young woman, and you are in your forties. You know where it is, how to get there, how to preserve your youth through this ... this escape. I knew it as soon as I saw you. I knew there had to be more in it than a simpleminded religious experience. ..."

He stopped when Margaret broke into laughter. His face was mottled in his fury. "You've been toying with us ever since this began. Why didn't Tyson publish? Why didn't he make any effort to share this great truth he had found?"

"Because he knew that it was there for anyone to find. Many have already. When the time comes, his proofs will be published and understood. But there is no hurry."

"Why did he suicide?" Bok's face drew near hers, and it was very ugly, red and livid at once.

Margaret swayed suddenly and caught the chair back for support.

The question had separated us again. The flow of information that I had gained from Paul and Josie was out of her reach and nothing was there to replace it. She felt only a blankness descend over her. I didn't believe Bok. Paul wouldn't have killed himself. Not Paul!

Morris Stein tried to take advantage of her sudden near collapse, almost automatically I shut him out, and he looked more puzzled and annoyed than before. In a faint voice Margaret said, "I've told you all I can now. The rest you have to get from the notebooks."

They left her soon after that. Bok and Morris Stein were arguing bitterly as they walked back to the garage apartment. I didn't think Morris Stein would be around very much longer, and I couldn't decide if I still wanted to punish him or not.

Margaret felt drained. She reviewed what she had told them and knew that it was all true, and with the thought she realized that she no longer knew what she meant by true. Real and unreal had become so close with borders so fuzzy and ambiguous that there was no way now to separate one from the other. True, untrue. How could she have learned anything about Paul Tyson and Josie when she had never met either of them, when all her information came from scrappy letters where certainly they didn't explain to each other what both already knew. She shook her head. But it was true.

Chapter 14

How had I got through to her? I knew that from time to time I had in the past, and I had done it again by supplying the facts that she needed to get rid of Bok and Morris Stein. How? How? All I wanted from her then was to be left alone long enough to play the scene as many times as necessary in order to catch the one clue that had escaped me before.

Margaret was very restless, as if she had been working too hard on a problem for a very long time, but a problem that she couldn't even identify. She decided that this was also a symptom of whatever it was that was wrong with her She understood that often people experiencing breakdowns complained of persistent fatigue and indecision. She wandered through the house, touching objects listlessly: the chairs where Paul and Josie had sat together talking in quiet voices; the couch where they had made love before the fire; the desk where he had sat working for hours. She stopped, staring at his chair, thinking if only she could have what they'd had together! Had he killed himself? She shook her head. She didn't believe it. She sat down at his desk and tried to recapture his presence as it had been in the hallucination, but nothing came of it. She wondered if it were possible for the house to be haunted, and she couldn't rid herself of the lingering suspicion that it was. The thought made her angry, but wouldn't go away. Ever since arriving in the house she had felt something, she had changed; everyone noticed the change even if she couldn't find it herself.

She decided to go out and work among the flowers again, and even that seemed foolish to her. Why, when she would be leaving in a day or two? Just because seemed a good enough answer. She weeded for the next hour, then found a trowel in the garage and transplanted seedling larkspurs to the middle of the early daffodils so that there would be continued bloom to look out on from the living room windows. After that she went down for a swim.

The water was icy, taking her breath away, and she swam straight out from the beach, to the end of the rocks that extended fifty yards. She was not in very good condition and by the time she reached the end of the formation, she was tired, her arms heavy and her breathing labored. She rested on the rocks, pulling herself onto one that dipped one end down into the water and was easily climbed. She looked back at the shore and it seemed farther than she remembered swimming. What if she had one of those curious little blackouts now, she wondered, would she simply remain here, or would she swim back with no memory of having done it? She thought about going mad, was it this kind of merger of reality with fantasy that she had been experiencing? In the end did fantasy win completely, and if so, did the person then living in a fantasy have a world less real than others who couldn't see it with him? She didn't know answers any longer, only questions. The sun warmed her again and she stood up, considering the swim back, or the alternate choice of clambering along the rocks back to the shore in bare feet. The rocks were upended out here, tilted crazily, with mossy patches, and fissures. Suddenly she wondered if Bennett had been right about the sailboat and its occupants: had they been real? Had a boat really hit the rocks only to free itself overnight? She looked for a scraped place on the granite blocks and found nothing. Gradually she became aware of a figure standing on the shore watching her. Morris Stein.

I was circling and slowly, or all at once, but only gradually becoming discernible, the day was different, the air hotter, the smell of the water suggesting an end of summer rather than a beginning. I was standing on the rocks watching, just watching. I saw Paul far out in the water, swimming, a speck of light hair, a flash of sun-burned arm. I was watching from a distance, but I was with him too. Closed circle, united with him, held securely by him, not afraid or confused, but regretful that something was ending. Not everything, just something, a phase was over, a new one to start.

No words there, but awareness, total awareness. Thoughts of love, the physical love and the love that came with the union apart from the bodies, thorough, complete, inseparable forever. Knowing with him when it was over. *It's all right, darling, it's all right.* No more fear or pain. Release, an end and a beginning. Circling joyously in union, a perfect blending of two beings.

"Josie! Come on in!" The voice brought me back. I stared at the noonday water and knew that the brief vision was ended. I turned around to look at Morris Stein and slowly nodded, and then slipped into the water and started to swim back. Very gradually Margaret and I separated again, but when we did, she knew the vision also, knew what had happened to Paul Tyson. She remembered feeling the agony of a heart that was being throttled and the joy at leaving the body that brought so much pain. She remembered the merger of two ... people who were not physically together, but much closer than mere touching could bring them. When she started to walk in the shallow water at the beach, she found that she was weeping silently. Not for Paul Tyson, or even for Josie who had been left alone, but for herself.

"You frightened me," Morris Stein said sharply. "You didn't even hear me, did you? I thought you were going to throw yourself in like he did years ago."

Margaret shook her head and wrapped her beach towel about her body. "What do you want now?" she said.

Morris Stein looked uncomfortable for the first time since she had met him. "I don't know," he said after a moment. Margaret started to walk up the stairs and he followed her, not speaking again until they had reached the top. "Can I come in and just talk to you for a while?" he asked. She glanced at him and he looked very young and very miserable. She shrugged.

Inside the house she left him in the kitchen while she showered and got into her clothes again. He had made coffee and sandwiches by the time she returned. He had a tray in the living room and was waiting for her. Before she could say anything, he said, "I have to apologize to you. And I don't know how."

She simply watched him. I was suspicious and on guard, but I didn't think he was playing a trick then.

"Look," he said, almost desperately, "Bok called me and told me what he thought he had. I got excited about it. Not that I believe in the other dimension, but because it fits in with what I am doing. That's no lie about the different ways of seeing the same reality, by the way. I am doing my thesis on it. But Bok made this sound like a gold mine for my research. Everyone who knows anything about physics and the study of time knows that Tyson thought he had something. I thought so. I leaped at the chance to get in on the perceptions he had recorded, not because I believed that he had found a way into another dimension, simply because here was the ideal chance to report a scientist's reactions to a distortion of reality." He stopped.

Margaret waited. Finally she said, "And?"

He shifted his feet and looked out the window at the patch of yard she had worked in. Daffodils were open there, a glare of dazzling gold shifting in the wind. He blinked. "I was willing to use you, use Bok, use Tyson's work. That isn't it exactly. I thought I had the right to use anything, or anyone. You know? But I didn't, and I'm sorry."

Margaret nodded, but he was still looking out the window. She sat down then and poured coffee for them both. She said nothing.

"I think I love you," he said suddenly. He swung around and looked at her with the hungry expression of an adolescent boy staring at his first fold-out nude.

Margaret shook her head, remembering how it had felt to be with Paul, wholly with him. She said slowly, "No. It isn't love. I don't know if you will ever love really, but if you do, then you will know that this isn't it."

I wondered if he knew about that one tiny touch that we had shared oh so briefly, if he realized that it could be so much more than that. He was shaking his head doggedly.

"I knew you wouldn't understand," he said miserably. "I took you and used you and made you do things, but that was a different me. I couldn't do that to you now. I couldn't use you in any way now."

"I know," Margaret said. "And you think that's love. Maybe reality has shifted, Mr. Stein. Maybe what you see now didn't exist several days ago. Maybe these distortions you speak of are not perceptual at all, but actual distortions, changes, in the reality that you take to be concrete and unchangeable."

He shook his head harder, but stood up. "I have to leave. Bok thinks my usefulness to him is at an end, and he ordered me out. I have to catch a bus. Can I come back? Can I see you sometime?"

Margaret hesitated. Soon she would be gone also. For him, Josie would have departed from his life. He would never find her again. She finally said, "I don't know how long I'll be here, or where I'll go after I leave."

He nodded. "And you won't get in touch with me ever. I know."

She never had seen anyone look quite so wretched. He stared at her another minute, then turned sharply and left. I heard the car leave soon after and knew that Bok had been waiting for him outside the door. Suddenly I realized that it had happened again, the blending of Margaret and me. When he had said he'd used her, she had known exactly what he meant, and she had accepted it calmly, with my memories of the entire scene, as if she never had forgotten it at all. She still had that memory, just as she had the memory of her talk with Bok and Morris Stein earlier that day, and her memory of feeling Josie's emotions out on the rocks. I felt afraid and exhilarated and uncertain and very puzzled about this merging that seemed to be happening, just happening.

Nothing else startling took place that day. Margaret remembered many things that she had forgotten, childhood incidents, attitudes of her parents and her brothers, her own attitudes that now seemed strange to her. She remembered scenes between her and Bennett and she marveled at her own ignorance, and his that was worse because it masqueraded under pretensions of knowledge. She called Gus Dyerman and placed an order for the makings of an extravagant lunch for her to prepare and take with John Llewellyn aboard his sailing boat. She slept deeply that night and awakened early feeling refreshed and eager.

She waited for John out on the rocks where he could bring in the boat on the side away from her beach. There was a slope on one side, but the other was sheer and straight and deep, a natural anchorage. She waved when the boat came into view and stood with the wind whipping her scarf and her hair under it until he got in close enough for her to step aboard, carrying the basket of food with her. They smiled, but said nothing, and he took the boat back out from the shore and headed up the island.

The land slipped away from them smoothly, the boat dipped, righted itself and dipped again, and it was another world suddenly. The wind was strong, billowing the sails, making the boat dance, making it feel as if they were deliberately restraining a living thing under their feet, a thing that wanted to be free to run with the wind. Margaret laughed aloud and John laughed with her. After two hours the land was behind them and only the sea stretched out before the dancing boat. The sun was hot, and the air clean and fresh and cool, and the lights on the water were alive and ceaselessly changing. The swells were very long and gentle, as if the ocean were breathing deeply and easily today, with no problems, just perfectly relaxed and contented.

John let the boat sway against the anchor while they had their lunch. They had not talked yet, but the silence that enveloped them was as relaxed and contented as the ocean itself. They sat side by side in the sun and when they were finished with the thermos of limeade that Margaret had brought, John took her hand and turned toward her. "I want to make love to you here in the sun," he said. She nodded. He went below and brought out a double sleeping bag that he opened, and then she started to undress. He watched her, not touching her at all until she was finished, and then he ran one hand lightly down her side to her hip, and holding her there, he tilted her head with his other hand and kissed her.

I had been in close all the while, searching for him, for something, almost hating her for what I knew was coming. She always found some sort of satisfaction for what was absent, even if she had to supply it herself, but I . . . I was empty too, and needed something, someone to share myself with, and there was no one. If sex could make me yearn as it did her, and then could fill the aching emptiness, I would have been content, would have tried to force her to find satisfaction more often than she did, but my yearnings were not sexual. Her body didn't have any effect on me at all, whether it hurt or was healthy and filled, it didn't touch me. When his kiss finished the undressing process, it was as if suddenly she became naked where before she had merely been unclothed. She was naked and exposed with no possibility of retreat even if she had wanted to retreat. All the hunger in her was there on the surface then, to be stoked and fed and kindled again and again. He knew. He was prepared for the immediate, all-over response. He caught her when she would have fallen; his hand on her hip slipped to the small of her back and pulled her to him, using his whole body as a crutch to steady her. His other hand pressed her head to him so that she was molded to him the entire length of her body.

"I know," he murmured. "I know."

"I dreamed . . . she started, and again he said softly, "I know. I was there." She sighed.

He undressed quickly and they lay together, his hands caressing her gently as he learned her body. He traced the bones in her shoulders, and her ribs and the sharper bones of her hips as she lay on her back. His gray eyes were steady on hers, and she finally closed her own eyes. He kissed each eyelid. He traced the outline of her lips, and then kissed them, and her mouth opened slightly and his tongue touched hers lightly at first, then harder. She wanted to say, take me now. I'm ready. She felt the tension in her body increase, a storm in her womb sent waves pounding through her faster and faster; her hands felt strange, almost numb, and even as she thought of them briefly her hands slipped away from her sides and touched him, feeling the lean hard body, wanting it on hers. She felt her frenzy increase when his mouth closed over her nipple and his tongue pushed in on the hard tip, followed it and pushed again making her feel as if a wire ran from there to her vagina, a wire charged, discharging. She writhed and her legs opened and she could feel the heat of the sun on her, and it seemed going through her.

I had withdrawn slightly, watchfully, but untouched, when suddenly I felt him. There was a shock that was as electric as that which she had felt when he bit her nipple. I was with him all at once, completely, and there was no way to get out again. Her pleasure with the flesh was nothing compared to this. There was total immersion in him then, his immersion in me, surrender and conquest that was inseparable, and every bit of me, whatever I was, was his, and he mine. This was the ecstasy that she sought and never had found, this the ultimate union that she suspected was possible, that she desperately wanted. I was something different than I had ever been before, bigger, better, beautiful and whole, completed from a half that had always been empty. And with this unity I knew his body, knew the ache in his bowels that only she could still now, and I knew her body too. I felt with her, and at the same time with him.

Margaret gasped as this new feeling swept her, and somehow from the time she started the convulsive catching of her breath and the time she actually drew in the air, I was Margaret, and I knew that John was a whole person, just as I was. I felt his body, the hard muscles in his back, the firm buttocks, and the firm hard penis that my body ached to receive. I knew his pleasure at my touch, and I wanted to prolong it, his and mine. He shifted and his mouth brushed my stomach, his lips caressing me as he moved downward. He brought his lips to my clitoris and I knew that I was shifting too then, eager for his kiss, just as eager to kiss him.

I marveled at the softness of the skin on the head of his penis and kissed it and he was kissing me also, his tongue playing with my clitoris, and each of us knew what the other was feeling. I knew his mixture of pain and pleasure when I grasped his penis and closed my mouth over it, and he knew mine when his tongue probed into me and the fire exploded like a volcano. Somewhere we both watched and knew and felt and were there too, and his laughter in my ear was of joy at being out on the gently swelling sea, with our bodies interlocked, sun hot on us, our inner beings as interlocked as the bodies. I moaned with the orgasm that shook me, and we both knew it was not over, but merely a plateau, that I would simply start at a higher point now. He kissed me again and his kiss was salty, and there was an odor that was exciting and made me more rhythmically under him. His hand left my breast and his fingers slipped inside my vagina and I came again as soon as he touched me, and I knew that I had to have him now. I had to have the release that only his orgasm could bring me, his and mine together. Everything else was preparation only for that moment, I knew, and it was his body that I was experiencing then, his need and urgency.

Somehow the boat was gone, and we were afloat over the undulating water, rising over the earth, sailing through filmy clouds freely, buoyant, effortlessly. We were blue air in a blue sky, interpenetrating clouds of raw nerves being exposed to impossible stimuli and being satisfied all at once. We were rising like water from a powerful fountain, sparkling, catching the sunlight in twinkling, glittering, flashing lights, and each spark was hunger and satisfaction together. The droplets merged and became drapes of the aurora, and the subtle shifts of colors were each of us, both of us winding about, through each other. We soared higher and were a rainbow of brilliance never surpassed though eternity might be searched, a rainbow with its parts so close that there was no separation of one hue from another, but only a blending. We spanned the earth, and then contracted to a shooting star, burning, burning, falling faster and faster, plummeting, a streak of light, a point hurling itself downward. Vertigo. Nothing.

"Meg, darling Meg."

I held his hand and we looked on the bodies still locked together, so still now, so beautiful. He smiled at me, and I knew that we were separating again, that I was becoming misty to him as he was to me, that my hand in his was like a warm, moist breeze. I wanted to reach out and catch him, and could read the same yearning in his face, even as he faded and became indistinct and finally was gone.

"Meg, darling Meg." She stirred and opened her eyes and stared at him in wonder. "Don't move," he said. "You are so very beautiful." He touched her cheek, and the same wonder that she felt showed in the way he touched her, in the awe that was written on his face. "You are so very beautiful inside, all the way through."

"I love you," she said then, and he nodded.

"I know. And I love you."

"There are so many things ... It won't be easy."

"It doesn't matter."

"I know."

Going back was dreamlike. The boat sailed over the water, and they were alone in a world that was lovely with a deepening blue sky, a sunset that was less vivid than the colors they had already experienced and had been. A moon rose that seemed almost to fill the sky, and the cool light turned the water into a black and silver dream image. At the rocks John helped her out, but didn't follow her.

"You have guests," he said, and she heard them too.

I circled once more, touched him briefly in a union that was sweeter and more poignant than the touch of the lips that she felt, and then he was leaving again. Margaret turned to the beach and the steps and saw Bennett waiting for her there.

Chapter 15

"My God, Margaret, what were you doing out there on those rocks? You must be frozen!"

"I'm fine, Bennett. When did you get here? I thought you weren't coming until tomorrow?"

"Arnold wanted to drive over tonight. He wants to talk to you. Betty is here, too. And I picked up Lizanne. Oh, and Shirley came along. It's a party, I guess. Lord knows where they'll all find rooms later on."

Margaret nodded and walked up the steps ahead of him. She stopped once and looked out over the water, but it was completely empty, with streaks of moonlight riding the ridges of the gently heaving water. There was no sailboat to be seen. Again she nodded.

"Arnold wants me to join the campaign, doesn't he?" she said, as they walked toward the house.

"I don't know what he wants. Nothing's going the way he thought it would, as it should. I just don't know. Maybe I'll pull out myself."

"You won't," Margaret said. She caught sight of Bok

starting to enter his car, and she called, "Dr. Bok, join us, why don't you? It's a party!"

He looked strangely at her, then smiled and nodded, too far away to say anything without shouting as she had done. In a moment he was with them at the back porch.

"Thank you, Miss Oliver. If you're sure I won't be intruding . . ."

"Of course not," she said. "You've met Bennett, haven't you? He has supplied the guests, the cook, the food. I might as well add to the festivities, don't you think?"

Bok looked at Bennett uncertainly, then back at Margaret. He seemed to be wishing that he had not accepted her spontaneous invitation. I could feel Bennett's anger with her, and I knew that Bok must be uncomfortable because of it. Margaret started to enter the house without looking back at him, and it would have made for an even less comfortable scene if he now decided to refuse her invitation. He trailed after Bennett.

"Lizanne, I hope this didn't catch you too suddenly, upset any plans," Margaret said to the gaunt woman. Lizanne nodded to her curtly and turned her attention back to the stove.

Margaret went on into the living room where Arnold Greeley was standing before the fireplace, holding a glass of Scotch and water in one hand, a cigar in the other, talking in a very fast, clipped voice to Shirley and Betty. He broke off what he was saying when he saw Margaret.

"My dear, we were all worried about you. How lovely you are looking."

"Hello, Arnold, Betty. Hi, Shirley. What a surprise to see all of you tonight. If you will excuse me, I will change and be with you in a few minutes." She knew her smile was too bright and didn't care. How ridiculous they all looked. Shirley's eyes were narrowed with suspicion and Betty Greeley had her mouth open to say something that Margaret didn't even wait to hear. She saw Bennett and Bok behind her and motioned them on into the living room. "You will introduce Dr. Bok to our guests, won't you," she said, and swept past them into the bedroom.

She showered quickly, humming under her breath, and when she was finished she found Bennett waiting for her in the bedroom. She smiled at him too. He looked as if he would like to feel her pulse, or something.

"Are you all right?" he asked. "Is anything the matter?"

"I've never been better," she said, pulling a long skirt from a hanger. It was a gaudy flowered skirt, and she put a white shirtwaist on with it.

"You look ... wonderful," he said, and his expression was the same one that she had seen on the face of Morris Stein. Suddenly she wished that he were there also. She brushed her hair quickly and coiled it high on her head and fastened pendant earrings to her ears.

"Rather gypsy looking, isn't it?" she said, studying her reflection. Her color was too high to add any more, she decided, and simply touched lipstick to her lips. Her nose was a bit sunburned, and the ridges of her cheekbones. Also, her hair was bleaching already from the sun. Bennett muttered something about returning to their guests and she smiled at him again in the mirror. He looked very puzzled.

Margaret finished and rejoined the group in the living room. She was not surprised to see that Morris Stein had come back and was even then talking unhappily to Shirley. He brightened when she entered.

"Mr. Stein, I was just wishing you were here for the party."

Bennett was mixing drinks and he handed her a glass. She sipped the drink, gin and tonic. She remembered gin and tonic at the inn, with Morris Stein. She raised her glass to him slightly and said, "Cheers." He looked unhappier than ever.

"Have you ever thought of concerning yourself with politics, Mr. Stein?" Betty Greeley couldn't bear not to use anyone who wandered into range. "I wonder how many politicians hire psychologists?" She pulled a notebook from her purse and made a note. "I'll find out," she said to her husband, who was looking at Morris Stein with interest.

"I hadn't given it much thought, no," he said. He looked thoughtful, however, and Margaret laughed.

Shirley said, "In this time of alienation, everyone really needs something that he can throw himself into whole-heartedly, and what could be better than politics for that fulfillment we all need? A real chance to do something for the country, for other people."

Margaret laughed and pretended to choke on her drink. She lighted a cigarette. She could hear the wind starting to blow now, and she thought of the sailboat dipping and swaying on the sea that was becoming choppy. "I'm sorry," she said to Bennett who was touching her arm.

"I said, you need something that is totally engrossing."

"Oh." She didn't pursue it. Bok had worked his way over to Morris Stein and they were whispering back and forth, neither of them waiting for the other to answer. They were both looking at Margaret; Bok kept shaking his head. Margaret raised her glass to them mockingly. I was watching Betty Greeley, and I knew that the woman was reappraising Margaret moment by moment. She was a purveyor of flesh, I thought, and she could judge it rather well. She was changing her opinion visibly.

Arnold Greeley said, "Margaret, we want you to join our group. We head into the Middle West next week, and we could use someone in our party who understands the people, speaks their language." His wife was trying to catch his attention, but he was watching Margaret now. Betty was pursing her lips hard at him, and he didn't see her.

"Oh, in what capacity, Arnold? What would I do?"

"Mostly be there. You know, campaigning isn't all speeches. We have cocktail parties, teas, luncheons. ... All you would have to do is be there, charming, friendly, with a Midwest accent ..."

Lizanne appeared and said that dinner was served. Margaret led the way to the dining room, talking now to Bok. "Is your work almost finished now? Are you really able to put together a comprehensive theory based on Paul Tyson's notes?"

Bok was staring at her as if one of them had gone mad and he hadn't yet decided which one. He pulled at his collar, running a finger under it again and again. "He left so many illegible notes," he said evasively and moved away from her to try to get nearer Morris Stein. Probably he felt that he had to touch someone he knew well. Morris Stein was staring at her too, not quite so openly, but with as much bewilderment.

Lizanne served them silently and efficiently. Chilled consommé sparkled like jewels and Margaret remembered the rainbow, and the aurora. . . . She was pulled back by Shirley's suddenly raucous voice.

"Margaret, what is the matter with you? Twice now you have simply not heard what we've said to you. Are you ill?"

"Do I look ill?" Margaret asked, wide-eyed. Shirley's face darkened in anger. "I'm sorry," Margaret said, knowing it was a lie, knowing that Shirley knew it was a lie. "What did you say?"

"I said that I would come over and help you get ready for the campaign next week. I have some books you should read first, and I'll coach you. . . ."

Margaret was shaking her head. "I'm sorry, I thought it was understood. I have no intention of going on the campaign trail with or for Arnold Greeley." She said it very simply, as if unable to understand that she hadn't made the point already.

Arnold Greeley stopped his fork midway to his mouth then put it down. "Why not?"

"Why should I, is more to the point."

"Because I need you. Your husband needs you with him. You can serve a useful purpose."

"My husband hasn't said that," Margaret said. "I don't believe he feels that he needs my presence on this tour."

"Margaret, of course I want you to go with us." Bennett was at the other end of the table, and he looked almost as angry with her as Shirley did.

"You want me to go with you," Margaret said thoughtfully. "You know that you don't need me, don't you? Not for that anyway."

"Not now," Bennett said. "Let's talk about it later." He turned to Arnold Greeley. "I'll explain it to her later."

Arnold Greeley was seated at Margaret's left. He looked at Bennett and said slowly, "Yes, you explain it to her, and you explain to her that no one in my organization can be disloyal to me, no one, not a single goddamned member of my team or the relative of anyone on my team."

Bok started to push his chair back nervously. He looked ill; his eyes kept coming back to rest on Margaret. He patted his napkin to his lips. "I think, I really must be on my way. I forgot that I have so much work . . ."

"Sit down," Arnold Greeley said. Bok turned to Margaret in confusion. She said nothing. "If you want to work with the stuff in this house, you'll sit down and keep your mouth shut," Arnold Greeley said. Bok sat down suddenly. Morris Stein had not moved during this. He looked to Margaret also. As before, she said nothing. Arnold Greeley said, to her now, "I can buy him and a dozen more like him." Morris Stein flushed, then blanched, and looked down at his plate.

"If you will excuse me," Margaret said then. She stood up and smiled faintly at Arnold Greeley, then turned and walked from the room. Bennett followed her.

I watched Shirley and Betty put their heads together, then heard the rustle of Betty's taffeta slip as she moved to Arnold's side. I lost the sounds when Margaret went into the bedroom.

"In God's name, what has come over you?" Bennett demanded, catching her arm, spinning her around.

"I really don't know," she said. She indicated the other room with a slight inclination of her head. "He's an evil man. I don't want him in my house again, ever."

"Your house! What are you talking about? He's my

guest, my employer. Margaret, you have to come along with us on this one trip. He's got his mind set on it now. That's why we came back here tonight. We have no one in our group who isn't from New England, and we need someone who can talk to the Midwesterners without ..."

Margaret put her fingers on his lips. "I know all about it," she said. "Believe me, I understand Arnold Greeley very well, and his motives. I won't go, Bennett."

Bennett pulled off his glasses and cleaned them thoroughly without speaking. When he had replaced them he looked at her and said, "All right. I told him that you weren't the type, that you are too shy for this sort of thing, not your cup of tea at all. I'll make him understand. ..."

Margaret shook her head. "You will quiet me for now, and come at me from another angle, won't you? Through my family, perhaps? If he hasn't already suggested that to you, he will. And you will go along with it because you like him, can't stand the idea that I might balk." Bennett was watching her with a mixture of suspicion and disbelief on his face.

"You know I wouldn't go along with anything like that," he said, very quickly, guiltily.

Margaret laughed again and walked to the window where she could see the moonlight shining in rays through the branches of the pine trees. "I'm going to leave you, Bennett."

"Margaret, for God's sake, what are you talking about?"

"I can't live with you any longer. I have to leave you, or else accept your reality, and I can't do that any longer. I don't like your reality."

"What the devil are you saying? What is that supposed to mean?"

"I think your world is a terrible place, and I've found myself accepting it again and again, as given, because I didn't know it wasn't all of reality. Now I know."

"You're losing your mind. You're talking like someone who's heading for a breakdown. . . ."

"You asked me once if there was another man . . ."

"I never did! It never would have occurred to me. . . ."

"Let's suppose that you did ask me, in another reality, and let's suppose that I said no. But there is, you see. Another man. I love him very much, and I can't live with you, sleep with you, share your miserable world with you now that I know what it can be like."

"Who is it? Bok? That kid with him, the psychologist? Who? How long?"

"I don't know how to tell you how long. In a sense forever . . ."

"Margaret, stop playing with me! Who is it?"

"Paul Tyson."

"I'm going mad, or you are, we both are. Margaret, you know Paul Tyson is dead! You know that! Why are you doing this to me? What have I done? I told you you don't have to go along with Greeley. I'll fix that. What else is bothering you? What have I done. Or said? I'm sorry for it, whatever it is."

"How can you say you're sorry before you know what it is? What if it's something that you think you're right about? Would you still say you're sorry?"

Bennett's jaw muscle tightened visibly. He said very quietly. "Tell me what I did and then let's talk about it.

You haven't given me a chance. You've just given an ultimatum. Why?"

"I don't think for a minute that you would understand my reasons. I told you that I don't like your reality and it is meaningless to you. You have no idea of what I'm talking about. You say that the man I love is dead, and I know he exists in someone else, just as a part of me exists in another, or many others. . . ."

"Darling, I know I've neglected you recently, you've been lonely, and I can't promise that there will be much improvement for the next few months. But be patient with me, darling. Please. After this is over, we'll go on a trip together, to Paris, Switzerland, Japan, wherever you want. We'll get a house in the country, with a garden. You'd like that, I know. I should have known someone as free and open as you are couldn't live in a city apartment year round. You should have said something . . ."

Margaret laughed suddenly. She hadn't wanted to, hadn't known it was coming until it was too late to stop. She said, "I'm sorry. I'm not laughing at you. At me really. I just realized how much larger your yard is than I'd thought before. Big enough to include a country house with a garden, and another trip abroad. But it's still your yard I'd be playing in, don't you see? Your wife in your yard, your property. I want to be free, Bennett. Can you understand that?"

"Free from what? My God, you've got everything a woman could ask for. Money, position, a faithful husband, security, freedom to come and go as you choose. . . . What more do you want?"

"I don't want anything. Nothing at all, and then I'll be free. And someday there will be a man who will make love to me and make me know that every bit of me is involved, every last bit, with nothing left over to look on from a distance. It, whatever it is, sits on my shoulder and laughs at your perfect, hygienic passion, just so long at this, then on to the next erogenous zone. You studied them, didn't you? You know exactly how long to work on every part, and in the end, there's nothing but hygiene and a quick grunt, and that observer has felt nothing. My body has done what it was supposed to do, and I feel nothing. Nothing at all. Empty. Used. Property."

"Margaret, don't talk like that! If you feel that our sex life is inadequate, we can discuss that, or see a counselor, or a doctor. ... But don't talk like a ..."

"Whore, Bennett? Is that the word? But don't you see, that's most of the problem right there. I suppose I feel rather like a whore, and no matter what you do, what you promise, I'll always feel like a whore with you. And it doesn't have to be like that."

"Christ, Margaret, we need time for this! Not now. Not with the house full of people. Give me time to think. Come on, let's go back now. I'll tell Arnold that we'll make a decision tomorrow, or the next day. Let's drop this for now."

Margaret smiled at him and nodded. "Yes, Bennett. We'll drop it."

He opened the door and held it for her. The others had gone to the living room with coffee by then, and they looked up curiously when Margaret and Bennett reappeared.

Margaret stopped at the doorway and looked at them. It was as if they were behind a transparent substance that she could walk through or not, but that they didn't know existed. She-I could see the whole of it from a place that was at once inside the room, and was at a distance from it, so that all of it was visible simultaneously. The shield no longer touched Margaret-me, and with the knowledge that it was gone, I sidestepped Bennett and went to the window. How had it happened? I didn't know. I looked at the sea, liquid silver moving restlessly under a steady wind. A streak of pale light touched the daffodils, and I could see it as a tangible thing that leaned from the sky to the ground, resting on the nodding flowers. I looked once at the people behind me, dolls, playing at being alive, and then slipped out to the streak of light, and let myself go up it, higher and higher. I wove around it, in and out of the cool light that bathed me and purified me and made me tingle with my own aliveness. looked for John, called to him, and when he didn't answer, I knew it was all right. He was out there, too, somewhere, and I would find him again, or he would find me. I knew that he was circling, just as I was, riding a moonbeam, free, without restraint, joyously alive. I looked once more at the living room, the dolls who ate and drank and spoke and didn't live at all. I pitied them and knew I could never return to them, under the shield that only they individually could pierce.

Margaret turned from the window and for a moment saw the others as I did, frozen in attitudes of laughing and talking, cups and glasses stopped. She moved and activity resumed in the room. No one tried to stop her and as she crossed the room, running her hand lightly over the back of the couch, promising to return one day. She was thinking of the moonbeams, and of John, and Paul's unfinished work. She knew that Bok could make nothing of it; he was incomplete. It was her work now, hers and John's. They would work together, and play together, and be one with the rainbows, fly with the wind, weave an aurora. ... She smiled inwardly, and she/I left the house, taking nothing from it, needing nothing from anyone there.